G FORCE

ANTHONY HAMPSHIRE is as comfortable strapped into the seat of a race car as he is in front of a classroom. Raised in London, England, and Calgary, Alberta, Anthony has been a racing driver and team manager, a football coach, and a magazine columnist. He was also a classroom teacher and educational technology consultant and is now a school principal. Anthony has earned national and provincial awards for his work in school curriculum and media, authored educational software, and is a regular conference presenter and workshop leader. He makes his home at the foot of the Rocky Mountains in Alberta, where he lives with his wife, two daughters, and a bossy Welsh Corgi.

Pace lap. A slow warm-up lap before starting the race.

Pace car. The official car that leads the race car field during the pace lap or a CAUTION PERIOD.

Pit. The area where teams work on the race cars.

Pit Board. A sign that is held up by the pit crew to inform their driver of place, race position, and lap.

Push. Another term for UNDERSTEER.

Podium. A stage where the top three race finishers receive their awards.

Pole position. The first starting position, which is awarded to the fastest qualifier.

Qualifying. Timed laps that determine where each car will be positioned at the start of the race.

Setup. Adjustments that are made to the race car by crew members.

Suspension. A system of springs, shocks, and levers that are attached to the wheels and support the race car.

Understeer. When the front wheels lose their grip and the race car continues straight rather than turning.

Undertray. A separate floor to the car that is bolted onto the underside of the main tub.

Wings. These direct airflow that passes over the race car, pushing it down onto the track.

G FORCE

Anthony Hampshire

Fitzhenry & Whiteside

Text copyright © 2009 by Anthony Hampshire

Published in Canada by Fitzhenry & Whiteside,
195 Allstate Parkway, Markham, Ontario L3R 4T8

Published in the United States by Fitzhenry & Whiteside,
311 Washington Street, Brighton, Massachusetts 02135

www.fitzhenry.ca   godwit@fitzhenry.ca

10 9 8 7 6 5 4 3 2 1

Library and Archives Canada Cataloguing in Publication
Hampshire, Anthony, 1951-
G force / Anthony Hampshire.

ISBN-13: 978-1-55455-027-2   ISBN-10: 1-55455-027-0
1. Automobile racing—Juvenile fiction. I. Title.
PS8565.A5663G19 2006   jC813'.6   C2006-906871-2

**U.S. Publisher Cataloging-in-Publication Data
(Library of Congress Standards)**
Hampshire, Anthony.
G Force / Anthony Hampshire.
[184] p. : cm.

Summary: Rising star Eddie Stewart is on the starting grid of the
Indianapolis 500, but a mysterious series of dangerous crashes threatens
to end Eddie's dream of winning at Indy before it even begins.
ISBN-10: ISBN 1-55455-027-0   ISBN-13: 9781554550272
1. Indianapolis Motor Speedway (Indianapolis, Ind.) –
Juvenile fiction. I. Title.
[Fic] dc22 PZ7.H367 2007

Fitzhenry & Whiteside acknowledges with thanks the Canada Council
for the Arts, and the Ontario Arts Council for their support of our
publishing program. We acknowledge the financial support of
the Government of Canada through the Book Publishing Industry
Development Program (BPIDP) for our publishing activities.

Design by Wycliffe Smith Design Inc.
Printed in Canada

To Maureen, Ali and Cait. You're still right.
—*A.H.*

Acknowledgements

I am very grateful to my tenacious editor, Christie Harkin, whose insights have made this a better story. Once again, I owe a special debt of gratitude to Ray and Leslie Mathiasen, owners of the Mathiasen Motorsports/RLM Investments Formula Atlantic team for graciously adopting me as a crew member, and for providing rare insights into the workings of a top professional race team.

A.H.

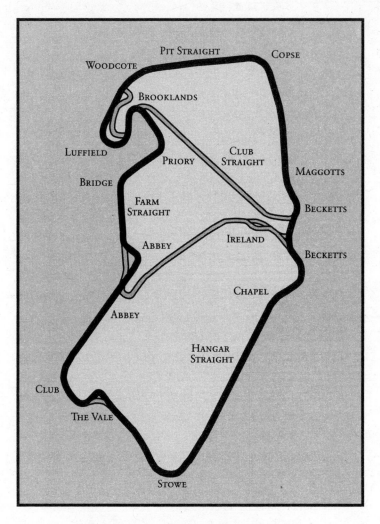

Silverstone Grand Prix Circuit
Length: 5140.11m (3.194 miles)

Chapter 1

Neck Pain

"Another new record on that last lap, Edward! Still P1. Plus 2:55. Last lap now."

I threw the Dallara Indy car into the tight left-hander before the main straight, snapped down two gears, buried the throttle, and kicked out the back end of the car in a huge power slide. I waved at the grandstand full of screaming beauty queens and celebrity photographers. Just like I'd done every lap of the race.

I straightened the car and punched the radio transmit button on my steering wheel.

"Sweet, Allan. Make sure the champagne is ready," I crowed.

My race engineer, Allan Tanner, had confirmed what I already knew. I was starting the final lap at the Gold Coast Indy 300 in Surfer's Paradise, Australia, in first place with almost a three-minute lead, and I had just broken the lap record. For the fifth time. Even though I'd never seen the track or driven an Indy car before this weekend, I'd had no trouble leading the field in practice, in both qualifying sessions, and in every lap of the race. I mentally rehearsed the speech I planned to deliver to the massive crowd from the top of the victory podium in a few minutes. "My DynaSport team gave me a great race car and my crew was awesome." Perfect.

I wound the shrieking Honda V8 up to the redline as I accelerated hard out of the hairpin turn. I was in the zone. Even above the roar of the engines, I could hear the crowd chanting.

Ed-die! Ed-die! Ed-die…

Suddenly, Surfer's Paradise started melting away, but someone was still calling my name.

"Eddie? Eddie?"

I slowly opened my eyes, focused, and realized, to my disappointment, that I was not strapped into an Indy car after all. I was slumped over in a train seat, propped up against the window. A kindly, older lady in the next seat was nudging my arm and smiling at me. I peeled my cheek off the window, straightened up in my seat, and worked the kink out of my neck.

"We'll be pulling into Victoria Station in about

twenty minutes, dearie," she said brightly.

"Thanks, Lizzie. Wow, London already!"

"You must have been very tired from your holiday in Kent. You fell asleep just a few minutes after we left Canterbury—didn't he, Harry?"

"Indeed he did, Lizzie," laughed her husband from the seat beside her. "I didn't even have the chance to ask you, Eddie. What is a nice young Canadian man, such as yourself, doing out in our neck of the woods, so to speak?"

"I'm a race car driver," I answered. "I was staying just outside Canterbury to do some physical fitness training at the Apex Training Facilities. Believe me, it was no holiday!"

Just a few months earlier, I had won second place at the North American Formula Atlantic Championship and Rookie of the Year honors. Those awards had caught the attention of some other race teams, and the phone had started ringing. During the fall, I'd picked up a ride in a Corvette for two races in California, co-driven a Porsche to a win at Road Atlanta, and even spent a week testing an Indy car in Florida.

Now I was traveling across England after three weeks at an intensive fitness-training boot camp. It was run by former special service commandos—and boy, were they tough. But it was a necessary part of my preparation for the latest racing project for my sponsor, DynaSport Industries. I had no idea what was up next and couldn't wait to meet with my race engineer, Allan Tanner, in the capital of his home country, London, England. Knowing Allan, I suspected that we were gearing up for something big next season.

"My goodness—a race car driver!" exclaimed Lizzie. "How exciting!"

"But why the physical training, Eddie?" asked Harry. "Don't you just have to sit in a car and drive?"

I rubbed my neck and chuckled.

"Oh, no, Harry. Driving a top-level race car is more demanding that most people think," I replied. "The Indy cars I was driving last fall taught me what serious G force means. See, 1G is simply the force of gravity on your body—the weight you normally feel just moving around. But put yourself in motion and this force multiplies. It doesn't matter if you're on a skateboard or in a race car: gravity is always there. And the faster you go, the more you feel its force. Imagine this: If you drive quickly in a normal car, your sunglasses slide across the dashboard, or you might spill your drink. If you're going hard in a really fast road car, you might get up to a force level of 1G, which is the same as your body weight. So, if you weigh 160 pounds it's like having another 160 pounds pushing into your side. Ever been flung around on a fast roller coaster? That's what 1G feels like."

"Oh, I used to love roller coasters when I was younger, but they're a bit hard on my back now," answered Lizzie, ruefully.

"Well, an Indy car is the best roller coaster ever invented for one person. It can generate over 1G under acceleration, 2Gs under braking, and 3Gs through a corner. At those levels, everything gets much heavier and harder to move."

"Going into those corners must be pretty tough," Harry whistled.

"I'll say," I replied. "You get crushed sideways like a lump of plasticene. Your engine is screaming inches behind your head and the G forces keep building up to the point where you can barely breathe."

"Not cars for the faint of heart," Harry observed.

"No, they're very serious pieces of machinery," I said. "And by the end of the fall, that Indy car had me beat. I was so tired that every time I carved it into a corner my head almost fell over. The crew fitted me with a padded collar but by the end of the last test day, my neck muscles were like Jell-O, and I actually had trouble holding my head up."

"Ah, yes," Lizzie said, with a wink at her husband.

"So we noticed."

Just then, a beep from my cell phone alerted me to a new text message.

Edward,
Meet @ Shakespeare Tavern. Tons to talk about.
Allan
PS: How's yr neck?

Chapter 2

What's Next

My new British traveling companions kindly gave me directions to the Shakespeare Tavern, just west of the station. There, I finally spotted a short, bald, deeply tanned fellow with a close-trimmed silver beard. He was sitting at a table by the window and waving at me.

"Over here, Edward!" Allan Tanner shouted through the noise of conversation and a soccer game on the big screen TV. He's just about the only person on the planet who gets away with calling me Edward.

I made my way through the dinner crowd, thinking how good it was to see Allan again. Since Allan is a fanatic for British history and culture, I wasn't surprised that he'd picked a tavern named for William Shakespeare, the famous British playwright and poet. He'd also thoughtfully ordered lunch for me: chicken and salad. Oh no.

"So, Edward you appear to have survived your three weeks in the country. Spectacular place, Kent. How did they treat you?" Allan asked.

"Pretty well," I replied, pushing my dinner slightly off to the side. "Once I got past the first week and got to know the guys better, I actually learned a lot."

"Do tell," Allan pressed as he poured the tea. Earl Grey, of course. His favourite.

I shifted in my chair to relieve my aching back. "Let's see, Allan. My trainers, Kevin, James, and Nigel, had me up before dawn. We ran fifteen miles cross country with heavy packs every day until I fell into bed at seven each night. And I lived on steamed chicken and salad for three weeks."

Allan laughed and sat back in his chair.

"So much for your dinner then. They must have decided to work on the psychological side as well. Putting up with all of that for three weeks would tend to test your endurance and your patience. They're very clever at Apex you know, and those ex-commandos know how to train people to face extreme situations. I hope you didn't complain too loudly or question their methods?"

"Nope, not a word. Well, maybe just once, at the end of the last day when they made dinner. They called it Bubble and Squeak."

Allan stopped pouring and looked at me.

"Day-old fried mash and veggies? Astonishing. That's very close to cruel and unusual punishment," Allan stated in amusement. "Well, if you got through the physical training *and* the Bubble and Squeak, I think that you'll be well prepared for what's next. By the way, how's the neck holding up?"

"I'm working on it every day," I replied. "Check out these muscles! With any luck I won't be able to button up my dress shirts anymore."

"Very impressive," Allan smiled indulgently. "As you know, Edward, J.R. Reynolds sees racing as a powerful way for the sports equipment DynaSport makes to reach customers around the world. He's very focused, he works hard, and he hates to lose. In any event, J.R. and I see those same qualities in you, Edward, which is one of the main reasons that you are under contract as our driver. He also shares your preference for seeing that things happen quickly. He wants to move the team up to the top level and he wants to do it this coming season. So, we've reached a decision. We're going to do Indianapolis."

I nearly choked on my tea.

"I'm going straight from Formula Atlantic to an Indy car? I know I just tested one but that's quite a jump," I protested. "Are you nuts?" Even though I had already guessed that we were moving up to big-time formula cars, I hadn't expected that J.R. would throw us straight into the deep end. And the Indianapolis 500 was definitely the deep end.

Allan grinned and leaned forward.

"You know, that is almost exactly what I said to J.R. in New York a month ago. He assured me that he was not. Impatient perhaps, but he is quite determined. He's done his homework and he knows what it will take to compete."

"But seriously Allan, we don't have the experience to do Indy," I said.

"Not necessarily," he replied. "The Indy 500 is one of the few sports events left in the world that still welcomes talented newcomers. Of course there are always the star drivers and teams who compete each year, but there are also the rookies who arrive every May from other forms of racing with a dream to race in the 500. And Indianapolis gives them that chance. There's one simple rule for everyone. If you're fast enough, you're in. So, we're having a go and announcing it on the website today. Of course it will cost a boatload of money. Plus, we'll need time to put the right people and equipment in place in order to get up to speed and qualify. But J.R. thinks we can do it. So do I."

My tea was getting cold as I stared into the distance, but it didn't matter. Getting a shot at the biggest race of them all tends to refocus your attention. And so did something else.

Squeezed into a corner on the other side of the pub was a short, heavy-set man in his mid-thirties, chattering away on a cell phone. Brian Holloway. The last time I'd seen Brian was a year ago in Toronto when he was working for one of my least favourite people, Raul DaSilva. Raul was an arrogant Brazilian multi-millionaire driver who had been kicked out of professional racing, along with his team, after he was caught cheating in last year's Formula Atlantic final. The information that led to his suspension had come partly from me, and Brian Holloway had been Raul's data engineer at the time. Brian had an impressive reputation in racing circles as a hired gun. He was a top data engineer who worked for the highest bidder. His ability to work with a race car's computer system and to access that system remotely made him a valuable team asset. Raul DaSilva's entire team had been made up of people like Brian who were smart but just there for the big money—and Raul had no shortage of money. What he didn't have anymore was a race team. And last I'd heard, Brian didn't have a job.

Brian finished his call, snapped his phone shut, and looked up at me.

"Eddie Stewart," he said coldly, as he walked by my table toward the exit. "What were the odds of running into you here?"

I smiled and extended my hand.

"How are you, Brian?" I asked. He simply stared at me in stony silence and stuck his hands firmly inside the pockets of his leather jacket.

"I'm over here on a short contract with an Italian team," he replied evenly. "It's been very hard since last season. Too bad, because I really liked my last job with DaSilva but it ended suddenly. Everything was going great and then—*BAM*—I was out on the street. I'm sure you remember, Eddie."

"We all have choices to make," I shrugged. "Anyway, good luck, Brian. Maybe I'll see you around while we're both over here."

"Let's hope not," he replied as he walked past me and out the door.

Chapter 3

The Deep End

ater that afternoon, Allan and I finally reached our new team headquarters in Brackley, about an hour's drive north of London, near the famous Silverstone racetrack. After we parked our Mini in front of a modern workshop, I walked in to find about 10,000 square feet of empty floor space. It was surrounded by a perimeter of empty work benches. We followed the sound of a lone voice coming from one of the two offices at the back. There, John R. Reynolds was sitting at a large table, which was covered with technical drawings and contracts, talking loudly on his cell phone.

"Eddie!"

Still gripping his phone, J.R. launched his six-foot-four-inch frame out of his chair and crushed my right hand in his. Even though he is the president of a sports equipment company that does over 400 million dollars in business around the world each year, J.R. is no desk jockey. He actually loves to use the skis, snowboards, and mountain bikes that DynaSport makes, and he still moves with the smooth power of a trained athlete.

It was great to see J.R. again. If he hadn't stepped in with sponsorship after watching me almost win my first ever Formula Atlantic race last year, I wouldn't have finished the season at all. I certainly wouldn't be getting ready to drive his car in the Indy 500.

"You look great," he said, after quickly ending his phone conversation. "The Apex boys were just telling me about your little visit with them."

"It was a long three weeks," I grinned, "but I made it. Man, they're tough guys."

"Yes, they are," J.R. agreed. "I like to use them for training inside the company, and I've also brought them in a few times to help us sort out some security problems. They're smart and very professional. So, as I'm sure that Allan has broken the news, tell me what you really think. Are you ready for the 500?"

I didn't answer right away, but not because I wasn't sure. At that point I knew that there was no way I was ready to lap the Indianapolis Motor Speedway at 220 miles per hour, but I didn't want J.R. to think I wasn't up to trying. I needed to stay employed.

"To tell you the truth J.R., I'm not ready. At least not

yet," I replied. "It's a huge jump up to an Indy car. We've never tried anything like a 500-mile race before, so there's a ton to learn. But I will promise you this. I'll work as hard as I know how and when May arrives, I'll be ready."

J.R. smiled, glanced at Allan, and winked.

"That's a good answer, Eddie. A respectful answer. Indy is a major challenge. It's a place that separates the pros from the amateurs, sometimes violently. And you're exactly right. We're not ready now, but we will be. I've thought about it a lot, talked to some knowledgeable racing people, and gone over the math. I think that with the talent we've got on this team and the right car, we're capable of giving it a shot. I wouldn't be taking a big chunk out of DynaSport's advertising budget to do Indy if I had any doubt about that."

Allan nodded. "When J.R. first approached me with the idea, Edward, I was not enthusiastic. Even with proper funds, entering the 500 for the first time and qualifying with a rookie driver is difficult. However, I do agree that we have a strong core of engineering talent, and I've seen what you can do with a good car. Provided that we build you one, I'm confident that you'll put it in the field."

"Agreed," J.R. said. "I've budgeted for the best equipment plus plenty of testing and practice time at the speedway. If we're going to the Indy 500, we're going to do it right."

"OK, J.R., I understand the commitment," I said. "But what's in it for you? We would almost have to win the whole thing for you get your money back."

J.R. shook his head. "Not really, not as long as you make the cut and qualify for one of the thirty-three starting spots. Once you're in the show, then the television exposure more than pays for the investment. The 500 reaches tens of millions of people around the world on race day, and every time our car is in a shot, the DynaSport brand is right out there with it. I couldn't buy that kind of TV advertising even if I wanted to. And the longer you run, the greater the exposure for us— especially if you're near the front."

"Cool!" I laughed. "It will be like driving a 200-mile-per-hour billboard. But why are we meeting at an empty shop here in the English countryside? The 500 is in Indianapolis, Indiana, and that's a long way from Brackley."

Allan motioned to the workshop space outside the office and said, "Let's take a quick tour. This facility offers more than just a fine workshop for our cars."

He turned to face me with a glint in his eye. As it turned out, he was preparing to take advantage of another opportunity to broaden my understanding of British history.

"At one time Edward, Brackley used to do a brisk

business in wool and lace, as did many of the old market towns in Northamptonshire. In fact, we exported a good deal of it to our colonies in North America. However, time and events passed Brackley by until professional motor racing arrived. These days, this town is better known as the headquarters of many of the top Formula 1 Grand Prix teams. One of them has a full-scale wind tunnel down the road, and I happen to know their team manager very well. And finally, Brackley is five minutes from Silverstone, site of the British Grand Prix and one of the fastest tracks in Europe. I think you'll find it quite an interesting place to test the cars when they're ready. Any other questions, Edward?"

"Yes," I replied. "I noticed you said 'cars.' As in 'more than one'?"

"He did," J. R. replied. "I bought an Indy car team last week. Transporters, tools, parts, everything. And three of the latest Dallara Indy cars. They'll be here next week."

Multiple Indy cars, a big dollar budget, F1 wind tunnels, and testing at Silverstone: this was way beyond anything I'd expected. It was going to take time to sink in.

Chapter 4

Wingman

I got the time I needed over the next month. Under Allan's direction, we transformed the cavernous Brackley space into a working race shop. It started with the arrival of two massive transporters containing three Indy cars and everything else a professional race team carries including parts chests, tools, stacks of wheels, pit carts, and refueling rigs.

Within a few short weeks, Allan and I had moved the cars and equipment into our shop. We set up two offices and a small area with exercise equipment to keep up my training. We'd even rented a farm house for our accommodations. All we needed now was the core of our team: Rick Grant and Herb MacDonald.

Rick, Herb, and I had been a solid team since our early days racing in Formula Ford. Together, we'd moved on to a Trans Am series Mustang, and then on to our run for the title in Formula Atlantic last season. The three of us had worked out a simple arrangement. Rick designed stuff, Herb built it, and I made it go fast. Aside from being my two best friends since junior high, they were also the only people that I completely trusted to work on my race car. To push everything right to the limit, lap after lap, I had to have complete confidence in the guys who put my car together. And if Rick and Herb had put their mark on it, I never worried.

Allan and I were doing paperwork in one of the offices when I heard them walk in.

Tall, skinny, and always on the go, Rick's boyish face and steel-blue eyes were framed by a small pair of wire-rimmed glasses. Whenever he removed these glasses and started to polish them, we knew that he had entered "turbo-brain" mode. He was one of those rare people who thought at light speed, saw beauty in math equations, and wrote computer software for fun. Rick liked nothing better than coming up with new ideas that always made our race cars faster, and we all knew that he was an excellent race engineer.

While Rick supplied the brains, Herb brought the muscle and a rare gift for understanding machines. He could make, build, or fix anything on a race car. He had an amazing ability to work round the clock for days on end if necessary, fueled by nothing more than pancakes and coffee strong enough to pave a driveway.

"The dynamic duo returns!" I yelled as I crossed the shop floor to meet them.

There was no reply. Instead, the two of them just stood there with their mouths open as they took in the new surroundings. Rick's eyes darted back and forth. Then he removed his glasses and started to polish them. Herb just gazed at the freshly painted floor, the new engine-assembly room, the gleaming work benches, and the two large offices. Plus the three Indy cars parked in front of him.

"Not bad Eddie, not bad at all," Herb declared. "Allan gave us the general idea in the car, and this looks like it'll do nicely. OK, where do I sleep?"

"Not here, for once," I replied. "We've rented a massive old house just outside of town. It's got eight bedrooms, a trout pond, and even some old stables out back. It was built in 1805."

"Does it have electricity and running water?" he asked. Herb was born and raised in Washington State and although he'd traveled in the States and Canada with our race team, this was the farthest he'd ever been from home.

I smiled. "Yes, it does. And a satellite dish, broadband internet, a sixty-inch plasma screen TV, and a kitchen stocked with pancake mix. This is a fairly advanced country, you know."

"How kind of you to point out the benefits of a few thousand years of civilization, Edward," Allan remarked dryly. "Herb, your tool chests arrived last week. Come along and I'll show you where we've placed them."

This left Rick standing alone in silence with his hands clasped behind his back, a pose that I had almost never seen him adopt before. He had replaced his freshly polished glasses and was staring into space, lost in thought. Rick's nature had many interesting sides, but quiet reflection was not one of them. In one smooth motion, he removed his over-coat, folded it carefully over his arm and began to walk slowly around the silent race cars. It was only then that I noticed what he was wearing.

His usual wardrobe of baggy jeans, Hawaiian surfer shirts, and sandals had been replaced by a green tweed jacket, red turtleneck sweater, white dress pants, and a shiny new pair of brown dress shoes. Something was definitely up.

"Pretty snappy outfit, Rick," I observed. "Is that what they're wearing on the beaches in the Mediterranean this year?"

I knew that he had been visiting his sister Caroline and my aunt Sophie, who were on an extended holiday in Greece, but I was pretty sure that they weren't responsible for this wardrobe makeover. They had taste, and a sense of color and style. Well, maybe not Aunt Sophie who liked to wear enormous sun hats with pieces of wax fruit attached to them, but Caroline certainly would never have let her brother out in public dressed like this.

Rick turned, narrowed his eyes, and smiled slyly.

"Hardly, my good man. I picked out this ensemble myself whilst in the city. London, actually. Rather dashing, if I do say so."

Slowly it came back to me. It was something in the way he pronounced "rather" and in his choice of words like "whilst" and "dashing." I'd heard this before, a long time ago. Wing Commander Grant of the British Royal Air Force had returned.

I had last seen this character when we were both in grade nine in Vancouver. While preparing a World War Two presentation for Mrs. Hale's Social Studies class, Rick became obsessed with the Royal Air Force and its fighter planes. He was right into it. I still had a clear image of Rick, in the role of Wing Commander Grant, standing in front of our class for forty-five minutes, dressed in a vintage flight suit and a leather jacket with a sheepskin collar.

"You know, Eddie, this is a cracking good jacket," he went on, admiring the material. "Saw it in the window, fancied myself in it, and thought, *Tally Ho!* Knew I had to have it. Popped into the shop, tried it on. Looked a bit dodgy at first, thought I was in for a bit of bother, but had a word with the chaps. They lengthened the sleeves, and now it's brilliant! After all, if you can't trust a London tailor, Eddie, then what's this old world coming to?"

This explanation was delivered in the worst British accent I'd ever heard. I had a good idea what Rick's world was about to come to if Allan overheard any of it. Fortunately, he was still helping Herb with his tools and was far enough away so that none of our conversation had reached his ears. I took Rick by the arm and walked him into the office area.

"OK, Wing Commander, it's time to drop the act," I stated. "It's even worse now than it was in grade nine, and trust me, certain people around here won't appreciate it. Allan's very proud of his culture and he's not going to be impressed if you're trashing the language."

Rick sighed and threw his coat over the back of a chair.

"You're sure Eddie? It's that bad?" he asked in his normal voice.

"It is," I replied.

"I just thought it would be fun to see if I could pull off the whole British thing," he explained. "You know, blend in like one of the locals, like I'd lived here all my life."

"With that accent in this part of the world, the locals would have you pegged for an imposter in ten seconds. Better save it."

Rick considered this for a moment and then said, "Maybe I could work on it now and then."

"No."

"Just a word or two?"

"Definitely not," I said. "Look Rick, we need you focused on engineering the car, not insulting the team manager, OK?"

"Yeah, OK," Rick replied. "Say no more. Don't like it though. Feeling a bit chuffed."

I held up my index finger as a silent warning, and he nodded sullenly.

I'd won that round, but somehow I suspected I hadn't heard the last of Wingman.

Chapter 5

Aero Head

To my relief, Rick kept his word and he dove straight into the challenge of preparing our three cars. It takes thousands of parts to build a complete Indy car and each one of them has something important to do. But it only takes one or two of them to fail before something goes wrong. We left nothing to chance and stripped each car right down to its basic carbon-fiber tub, checking all the parts and making lists of what needed to be replaced.

After days of going through everything thoroughly, we were confident that the cars were in excellent shape. Rick, however, was always looking for an edge over the competition. Lately, he had been spending a lot of late nights on his three laptop computers. I had a strong feeling that he was working out something new. Still, I knew better than to ask him about it until he was ready. Rick loved to surprise us.

Allan, meanwhile, had been busy putting together his own surprise.

"Gentlemen, we have a new engine deal," he announced over tea one afternoon. "Three weeks ago, I had a call from EuroTech Engineering in France asking me about our Indy project. It turns out that they are interested in the 500. I now have an agreement with EuroTech to use their engines and their management software. I'm rather pleased, actually," he said with a bright smile.

He had every right to be pleased. EuroTech had a well-earned reputation for building engines that were tough as anvils while delivering enormous power and excellent fuel mileage. Just what we needed for 500 miles of full-throttle racing.

"Wow, I'm seriously impressed," said Herb. "EuroTech has built awesome engines for some Formula 1 teams, but I don't think they've ever done Indy."

"Quite right," Allan replied, "which is why they contacted us. I told them that we had some interesting new ideas. So, after a bit of negotiation we struck a deal. They're going to assign one of their engineers to work with us here, and we should see our first shipment of engines arriving just after Christmas."

"Wait a second. Sounds like there's some stuff going on that we haven't heard about yet. Is that right, Brainiac?" Herb asked, looking directly at Rick, who was tapping out some commands on his laptop.

"Well, yes," Rick replied. "I wasn't sure if it was going to work at first, so I didn't want to say too much, but I think I've got it figured out now."

Rick turned his laptop so that we could all see the screen clearly. The display showed a large, lime-green blob that changed shape as it slowly floated across a black background.

"Cool retro screen saver, Rick," I said. "It's kind of a lava lamp thing."

"Yeah, I know what you mean, Eddie," he replied. "When I wrote the code for this application I didn't expect it to look so squishy. Anyway, forget what it looks like. What this is really about is computational fluid dynamics or CFD for short. I've set this software up to analyze how a solid object behaves when it moves through the air. It figures out all of the pressures and speeds on and around whatever object you choose. The air is this green blob, and here is an object."

Rick tapped a few keys, and a silver three-dimensional model of an Indy car appeared in the middle of the floating blob. A few more clicks and the blob changed into a smooth stream of green liquid flowing past the car.

"I've worked out how to compress the information and convert it to graphic form," added Rick. "So now, not only do I get the numbers, but I can also actually see how much lift and drag this model creates as it moves through the air stream model at say, 250 miles an hour."

"Wow, that'll be handy for Indy drivers when they hit a patch of green Jell-O on the back straight," Herb remarked.

"Hilarious as usual, Herb," Rick replied coolly. "Remember: the green fluid on the screen is simply air—let's say Indianapolis air. I can put a model of our car, or any part of it, into this stream and see how it reacts in fast-moving air. We can tell how aerodynamic it is. It works with any object."

With a mischievous grin, he grabbed the computer mouse.

"Allow me to provide a short demonstration. Now, let's see. I need to find something really thick and dense." A moment later, he leaned back from the screen.

"Perfect," Rick said.

Rick had cropped Herb's head out of one of our team photos, converted it into a three-dimensional model, and placed it in the middle of the green stream.

I glanced sideways and caught Herb's eye. He wasn't smiling.

With a few more keystrokes, Rick started to accelerate the green air stream past the 3D model of Herb's head.

"Now as you can see, at a speed of thirty miles per hour, old Herb is pretty aerodynamic. The air stream flows smoothly around him. No turbulence. But as we accelerate the air speed to say, 100 miles per hour— well, now things aren't very smooth at all. The air is swirling around everywhere, and the pressures on the graphs are much higher. Notice that Herb's glasses have blown away and that his eyelids are starting to peel back. He is not getting through the air at all well."

"I guess I'm just not an aerodynamic guy," Herb growled.

"No, Herb you're not," Rick agreed. "And I predict that it will get a lot worse as the speed goes up."

Three more clicks and we were at 250 miles per hour. It was scary.

"At this speed, Herb has some very severe aero problems. His lips and cheeks have been blown back close to his ears. His nose has been flattened and, yes, we can see his hair is blowing away in small patches. But also look at what the air around him is doing. We now have major turbulence as the air tries to get around his head. Very unstable."

"So, Herb, do you want to go for 300? You might look good as a bald guy," I said.

"I think that will do for now, lads." Allan grinned and slowly closed the lid of the laptop. "Rick has done a fine job for us here. With this software, we have a way to design our car on the computer, model how it moves through the air, and actually see what it'll do at any speed up to 250 miles per hour. We can design parts that create the best combination of lift, drag, deformation, pressure, and so on before we actually build anything for real in the shop."

"But if we don't get to build and test these new parts, where's the fun in that?" Herb asked.

Rick polished his glasses as he answered. "The fun comes in not having to build stuff that won't work, Herb. Say that we spent weeks building a truckload of different wings, undertrays, and side pods that we think might be good. But we can't really know until we test them out on the car. So, we take them all to the track, bolt the first one on the car, send Eddie out, collect the data, bring him in, ask him what he thinks, take it off, put on the next one, and do that over and over again until we find the one that works—if we're lucky. In the end, they might all turn out to be useless."

"And your software solves that?" I asked.

"It should. With this program, we can build and test dozens of designs in a few weeks instead of months. If the design doesn't work on the computer, then we know that it's not going to work for real. So, we simply delete it and try something else. We can figure out the best combination from the software models first. Then we can actually make parts that we know will work."

Allan nodded. "This software should be almost as accurate as actual testing. Don't despair Herb—we have the time to do both, so you'll be busy enough at your workbench. Once we narrow it down to a few good designs, you'll build those. Then we'll run them in the wind tunnel to fine tune the aero balance. Finally, we'll go to the track and see which combination young Edward likes best."

Rick had been looking for an edge for us and he'd found it. Again. We would be able to arrive at Indy in May with a superbly aerodynamic car—and at over 200 miles per hour, that kind of structural advantage would be of critical importance.

Like aircraft wings in reverse, a race car's wings, undertray, and side pods work together to generate the downforce necessary to keep the car firmly planted on the track. Without enough downforce, the car can lose grip and, in a heartbeat, crush itself against the thick concrete wall that rings every inch of the Indianapolis Motor Speedway. An impact at that speed isn't the sort of accident that many drivers walk away from. With Rick's new computer-simulation approach, I wouldn't have to find out the hard way what would work and what would not.

"OK, I'm sold," Herb said as he got up from the table. "Just one thing, Rick. Put my head back."

Chapter 6

Christmas with Sophie

During December, six EuroTech engines arrived—the perfect Christmas present for Herb. He immediately took one of them completely apart in the engine room, humming happily, while the rest of us started to build the test car. We were so involved in the work that we lost track of the days; before anyone realized it, the morning of December 19th had arrived. And so did my Aunt Sophie.

She came through our shop door, slammed it behind her, and spread her arms wide.

"Surprise! Hello, my boys! Merry Christmas!"

Sophia Novello is a very large and powerful middle-aged woman, just over five feet tall and almost as wide. She's my great aunt, proudly Italian, and full of energy. Normally she wears loud floral dresses and enormous sun hats, but this time she was dressed for an Arctic expedition with a fluffy, black fur hat, a matching full-length down parka, a long, white silk scarf, and yellow snow boots. At a glance, she might have been mistaken for a penguin, except for the sparkling brown eyes and brilliant smile that radiated from her round, deeply tanned face.

We instantly dropped what we were doing and rushed over to greet her.

"Eddie!" she exclaimed as she wrapped me in a bear hug. "And Rickie...and Herbie!"

She crushed Rick like a bread stick, and then turned to Herb, but he just lifted her a foot off the ground and planted a noisy kiss on her cheek before setting her down. After I lost my mom to cancer when I was fourteen, Aunt Sophie had stepped in and helped my dad and me through a very dark time. When we started racing, she immediately adopted Herb and Rick as well. We became "the boys," and the three of us loved Sophie to bits.

"Welcome, Sophie," Allan said as he stepped forward and received his more formal hug like a gentleman. "This is an unexpected pleasure. Rick told us you were in Greece."

"I was. It was warm and sunny, and of course I look marvelous. Caroline and I had wonderful shopping in the little villages. But now she has gone back to her university. Rickie told me that all of you are here in this freezing country. So, it is Christmas and I am here. I have brought presents. And I wish to cook."

We moved Sophie into the manor house, and I took her into Brackley for the day to get "supplies." We stuffed the Mini with enough pots, pans, kitchen equipment, and groceries for a small army; picked up boxes of Christmas decorations; and lashed a spruce tree to the roof. By the time Allan, Herb, and Rick arrived from the shop, I had the tree up and decorated. Sophie, meanwhile, was happily stocking the kitchen in readiness for the Christmas dinner she planned to spend the next three days preparing.

"Excellent tree, Eddie. Hey, there's presents!" Rick exclaimed.

Sophie had placed gifts for each of us under the tree, and I noticed that there were also presents for all of us from Caroline, Rick's younger sister. They both had the same blond hair, deep blue eyes, sharp intellect, and bizarre sense of humor. But unlike her brother, Caroline had common sense and the organizational skills to run a small country. And she was gorgeous. Rick thought that we had "a thing" for each other.

I'll admit it: Rick was right. Ever since last season, when his tall, skinny, kid sister had come back from three years at art school, I'd been barely capable of speaking to her in complete sentences. She had blossomed into an athletic supermodel who looked as if she belonged on the cover of a Paris fashion magazine. I was stunned.

Caroline instantly found my reaction hilarious, but fortunately for me, we discovered that the feelings were mutual. Now that she was back at university for the year in a film and television program, we kept in touch through email. But I still missed her.

Allan announced the next morning that the team was officially on Christmas holidays. The next few days were spent in a flurry of shopping (us) and baking (Aunt Sophie).

Sophie had everyone up early Christmas morning for a full English breakfast. Only once the last bit of fried eggs and sausages had disappeared were we allowed into the living room where she had hung individual stockings for everyone filled with tangerine oranges. We opened our gifts and spent the afternoon singing carols and playing poker for walnuts.

The day came to a satisfying close after the best Christmas dinner I'd ever had, complete with noise-makers, paper crowns, and the type of pancakes that you're not supposed to set on fire with brandy. But Herb did anyway.

Chapter 7

Konrad

Christmas had been a welcome break, but starting a brand new year got us back to business quickly. The racetrack at Silverstone opened in February, and the next six weeks of preparation flew by. I doubled my workout schedule. Our team put Rick's CFD computer model to the test and narrowed down the car's aerodynamic design to three optimal setups. Then Herb built the test cars, and we took them to the nearby Ross Grand Prix Engineering facility to test them in the wind tunnels.

After watching the car inside the tunnel through the glass wall of an observation room and following the readouts from the instruments, the engineers were impressed. The first test run clearly demonstrated that the design was creating serious downforce, and doing it without adding a lot of drag from the front and rear wings. The design wasn't totally perfect, but it was pretty close.

After three days of fine tuning in the wind tunnel, Rick and Allan were both satisfied. "I don't always put a lot of faith in computers as you know, Rick," Allan said, "but these results are excellent. Well done, indeed."

Rick grinned. "Thanks, Allan. The air was all over the place in the old design that came with the car, but now it's smoother with way more downforce. That should make it easier to drive."

"And more stable in traffic," I added. "We're going to need that with thirty-two other cars out there."

I'd had some scary experiences with "bad air," which is what a race car gets when it's tucked in close behind another one. Imagine one speedboat following another and sitting right in the first boat's wake. The water is choppy and rough, and the second boat has a really hard time staying smooth and stable. Substitute air for water, and race cars for boats, and up the speed to 200 miles per hour, and you get the same effect. At that speed in turbulent air, the car loses downforce, loses grip, and starts to float and wander around all by itself. Not a happy feeling when you're covering the length of a football field in less than a second. However, a car with a very good aero package will remain stable in choppy, turbulent air even in heavy traffic.

We brought our car back to the shop, confident that we had an aero setup that would allow us to lap the track at competitive speeds with a stable car, and that we had a powerful, reliable engine. With these two critical pieces in place, we were almost ready to put the test car on the track for the first time.

Yet another important part of our plan for success was on his way, as well. EuroTech had promised to lend us one of their engineers to assist with the testing at Silverstone, and he arrived with Allan as we were loading the car into the transporter.

"Gentlemen, allow me to introduce Konrad Andersen from EuroTech. He'll be working with us from today forward," Allan announced.

Konrad appeared to be in his late thirties, with a quick smile and a slim, lean build. He struck me as a quiet but likeable guy.

Allan took him for a tour of the shop while Herb and I started to load the first stack of new wheels and tires into the back of the transporter.

"I thought Allan said that EuroTech was just lending us their guy while we're here in England. Sounds like he's on board with us for Indy too," Herb said.

"Looks that way," I replied. "Well, it never hurts to

have another engineer around, right Herb?"

"If you say so. I just hope he's got his head in the game and doesn't plan on standing around watching. Or trying to interfere with Rick. There's a lot of hard work ahead and we need a guy who's a team player and ready to get his hands dirty. Like Rick."

With his tour complete, Konrad casually walked over to me with his hands in his pockets. Herb came out of the transporter to join us.

"This shop is very impressive, Eddie," he said. "Do you all stay here?"

"No, we've got a big house just outside of town. Lots of room for you," I replied.

Konrad shook his head. "Thank you, but the company has already rented an apartment for me in town. I will need to travel back and forth between here and France quite a bit, and my assignment will often require me to work through the night on the computer network."

"So what did EuroTech tell you about this project?" Herb asked, leaning against the tire stack.

"They said that you would be using our newest 811B V8 engines, and I see that they have arrived. I am to set up a network here, and then assist you with the car's onboard computer and the software that we use to control the engine's critical functions.

EuroTech is especially interested in fuel efficiency. We believe that a 500-mile race will give us valuable information about how to increase this through the use of our fuel-mapping software. That is my specialty. This knowledge will be very valuable for racing and also for motorists because of the price of fuel these days."

There was an accent in Konrad's speech that I couldn't quite place, but it definitely wasn't French. His English was almost textbook perfect. He pronounced each word more clearly and carefully than any of us did, as if he had been formally taught English in a classroom rather than learning it in daily life.

"Have you ever worked with a race team before, Konrad?" I asked.

"Not directly. Usually I am in the office or in the test lab. I have worked on the racing cars that have come to the EuroTech shop and gone to the track for testing. But I have never attended the races. It looks very dangerous."

"Well, this sport is unpredictable, and it can be scary," I said. "But it's also the most fun I've ever had. If you like competition and extreme machines, there's nothing like it."

"Actually, Eddie, I am a terrible driver. I prefer to

jog or cycle to work. The traffic is too hard on my nerves and it makes my stomach ulcer act up." Konrad glanced around. "Now, may I help you with the rest of these tires?"

"No, we're good," Herb said. "But I want to pick your brain about those engines later."

"Give me a day or two to set up the network in the engine room, and I will be happy to help you," Konrad replied.

Herb and I looked at each other for a long moment as Konrad quickly walked away. Neither of us said anything but I was pretty sure that we were both thinking the same thing. Konrad wasn't a gear head like the rest of us, but he seemed knowledgeable, positive, and helpful. If he proved that he could be a team player, and if we could get him used to Herb's coffee, he just might work out.

Chapter 8

Silverstone

Modern Silverstone is the home of the British Grand Prix and a popular test track for many Formula 1 teams. While Herb, Rick, and Konrad were getting the car unloaded and setting up our pit equipment, Allan drew me a detailed map of the track and explained why he had chosen Silverstone.

"First of all Edward, I've tested cars at this circuit many times and I know what it demands. Parts of it are very fast with a top speed of over 180 miles per hour. Not as fast as Indianapolis, mind you, but we will be able to test all of the critical systems on the car. This will give us a good baseline for Indy in May. But what's more important right now is to find out how strong this car is and to expose any weaknesses. This Silverstone track requires rapid changes in speed, which puts a lot of stress on all of the mechanical parts. After pounding out almost 1,000 race miles on this car, we'll know where the weak spots are and what needs to be strengthened well before we get to Indy."

Allan didn't mention it, but I knew that one of the parts that was due for a good 1,000-mile pounding was going to be me. Just looking at the track diagram, I could tell that this place would generate some very high G forces. I automatically started rubbing the back of my neck as I studied the track layout.

"OK Allan, tell me what to look for."

He took out a pen and pointed to the start/finish line.

"As you cross the start/finish line here, you will be flat out in sixth gear and will likely touch 180 miles per hour before braking and shifting down two gears for the right-hander at Copse. Then it's hard on the throttle and—"

"Just a second," I said. "Did you say *cops*, Allan?"

"Yes. Copse corner."

"*Cops* as in the police, or *copse* with an 'e,' as in a grove of trees?" I asked.

"A grove of trees."

"So there are trees on this corner?"

"No."

"Why don't they just call it 'Turn 1' then?"

"I don't know, Edward. Perhaps it's just the English. We like to name our corners. May I continue?"

"Yes, OK. Sorry."

"All right then, through Copse you will feel G forces of close to 3.5, so this is where your months of training will pay off. Then up to top speed again before you go into Maggotts, a tricky left/right combination and—"

My hand was up again.

"Maggotts?" I asked.

"Yes, Edward, Maggotts. And I can assure you that there are no slugs, worms, or caterpillars in the area. Shall I write down turns 2 and 3 instead?"

"Please."

"Right. So, out of turns 2 and 3 and then through Becketts, or turns 4 and 5, on to Chapel, turn 6. Now listen Edward, turns 2 through 6, Maggotts-Becketts-Chapel, is a combination that is extremely demanding. You must flick the car left, then right, shift down two gears, and then accelerate hard through a fast right while fighting over 2Gs of lateral force. Then up to top speed again on Hangar Straight but no chance for a rest because the next corner, the right hander at Stowe, comes up fast."

"So, that's turn 7?"

"Correct."

Allan carried on and I did try to pay attention, but he lost me in the rest of the names like Vale, Club, Abbey, Brooklands, Luffield, and Woodcote.

"So, there you are Edward. A lap of Silverstone. Any questions?"

I shook my head. The map was a good starting point, but what I really needed was to get out there and start learning the track for myself. I glanced over at the car and noticed that the guys had completed their detailed checklists, which we always use to make sure that everything is right before the car ever turns a wheel on the track. Rick had just finished putting in the fuel and Herb was preparing to put on four new tires. That was my cue to slip into the transporter and put on my driver's gear: an inner layer of fireproof long underwear, a turtleneck, and thick socks; an outer layer of my dark blue, triple-layer driving suit and lightweight driving shoes; and some new red gloves Herb had given me for Christmas. I added a hood with an opening for my eyes, then my helmet, and finally a head and neck brace.

None of it was especially comfortable or stylish, but it was all fireproof and that's what counted. If I was ever trapped inside a burning car, this suit of clothing would give me about a minute of extra protection so I could get out.

I heard the high-pitched whir of a starter motor and then the explosive snarl of the EuroTech V8 coming to life.

"Nothing like the sound of 800 horsepower on a chilly morning, Edward," Allan said as I stepped out of the transporter. "Do you remember what I once told you before your first Formula Atlantic race?"

I smiled and nodded. "Like it was yesterday. First time in a new car on a new track. I'll be careful."

"Good lad. This isn't a race weekend, but there are some other teams testing, so keep a sharp eye on your mirrors. The tires are stone cold and it's cool today, so it will take much longer than usual for them to warm up and provide decent grip. Very gentle on the throttle to begin with, then nice and smooth through the corners. Give me ten easy laps to get some heat into the tires, then I'll call you in to make sure everything's all right."

I hadn't been in a race car for a while, but all the familiar noises, vibrations, and sensations came rushing back immediately. It was great to feel that urgent wall of power at my back again as I took the car carefully up through the gears.

I was tempted to unleash it during those first ten laps, but I followed orders and gently found my way around Silverstone, letting everything warm up, getting used to the controls, and watching the mirrors. Although I had seen a few other cars in the pits, so far I had the track to myself.

"OK Edward, bring it in," Allan directed through my helmet's headset.

I brought the car into the pit lane, saw Herb waving, pulled to a stop, and shut the engine off. Konrad immediately stepped to the side of the car, balancing a laptop on one hand, while he plugged a cable into the data port behind the cockpit and uploaded information from the engine computer. Rick and Herb were busy writing down tire temperatures and checking wing settings. Allan passed me a water bottle, checked the digital readout on the steering wheel, and kneeled beside the car.

"Everything feel all right?" he asked.

"Feels great," I replied. "I'm still not always sure which way the corners go, but I'm getting it. Can I open it up a bit?"

Allan shook his head.

"No, Edward," he replied firmly. "If this was a race weekend then we would be looking for speed, and I know that you would like nothing better than to put your foot down. But this is the first day of a test program, and we're after different things. The electronic sensors throughout the car will record very detailed information from the suspension, steering, throttle, brakes, and so on. We need to collect as much of that data as we can, so you must keep your driving style consistant and do everything the same, lap after lap. We almost need to eliminate you as a factor and just focus on the car, so that if a change made it faster or slower, we'll know it wasn't you speeding up or slowing down. For the next few weeks you need to think like a test driver. Not a racing driver. Get comfortable with your car, and try to make every lap identical."

"Understood," I said, handing him back the water bottle.

Konrad removed his data cable and joined Allan as they stepped away from the car.

"All right, Edward, you have nearly a full tank of fuel. Get up to speed and let's give it a nice long run."

Herb hooked up the remote starter. I fired the engine, gave the guys a thumbs-up, and rolled down the pit lane.

It was time to go to work.

Chapter 9

Lady Caroline

W e logged over 200 miles on that first test day, and after the initial rush of lapping Silverstone in an Indy car wore off, it almost became routine. There was no crowd of spectators, very little traffic on the track, and none of the frantic energy of a race weekend.

For the rest of February, with constant track-testing three days each week, I learned every bump, tar strip, and curb so well that I probably could have driven Silverstone in the dark. Driving an Indy car is always fun, but the constant high G forces still left me tired and sore at the end of each day, even after all those hours in the gym. We always followed the same routine and completed each day by sitting down after one of Sophie's fabulous dinners. Then, we'd look at the data and discuss what we had discovered and what new ideas we might try.

We were all impressed with how easily we could use the testing data on Konrad's new computer network. He knew at least as much about data and computers as Rick did, and he actually seemed to enjoy helping out in the shop. He still didn't talk much, but he was a bright guy who picked things up the first time, worked hard, and made useful suggestions. And his engines were performing flawlessly, producing excellent power and fuel mileage.

After almost three weeks of testing, the time to see what the Dallara car could really do finally arrived. In Allan's opinion, we knew enough to start work on race setups. We put a fresh engine and gearbox in the car, loaded up four sets of the latest Firestone slick tires, and arrived at Silverstone ready to find some speed. For a change, I saw that we had some company. And a familiar face.

Scuderia Fillipetti, an Italian Formula 1 team, had arrived for some testing of their own and had set up next to our pit area. Konrad and I were having a very close look at their new car, and I was hoping that at some point we might both be out at the same time. I really wanted to have a chance to see how the performance of our Dallara Indy car compared with

F1 technology. I was running that movie through my head when my old buddy, Brian Holloway, stepped out of their transporter.

"Hey, Brian," I said. "Here we are again. And you're with a Formula 1 team. Pretty impressive."

"What is it with you, Stewart?" Brian snapped. "You just keep turning up and spoiling my day."

I shrugged. "Well, there's no better place in England to test race cars than Silverstone."

"Yeah, thanks for the tip," he replied. "So what are you driving?"

I nodded in the direction of our gleaming white Dallara which had attracted the attention of the Scuderia Fillipetti mechanics.

"That's our Indy car," I said.

Brian shrugged it off.

"OK, look Stewart, I'll make this simple. I used to have a great reputation as a race engineer, and I intend to get it back. I've been hired for a month of testing with this team. A Formula 1 team. So it's a serious deal. I'm going to do great work for them, find them some real speed, and then the word will get around that Brian Holloway is back in the game. By the time I return to the States, I'll be in demand again. But there's just one problem," he said.

"What's that?" I asked.

"You. You're bad luck for me, Stewart. So do yourself a favor, OK? Just make sure that you and that Indy car stay out of my way."

Konrad had been watching this exchange, and he started chewing his thumbnail as we walked back to our pit area.

"Eddie, what's wrong with that man? It sounds like he just threatened you."

I shook my head. "No, that's just Brian Holloway. It's always about him. He likes to talk big and try and get inside your head. Don't let him get to you. I sure won't."

We returned to our pit to find that Herb had finished putting on our new tires and was warming up the car. I changed into my driving suit and then sat down with Allan and Rick to go over the plan for the day.

"Wasn't that Brian Holloway you were just talking to?" Rick asked.

"Yeah," I replied. "He's doing some computer work for the Fillipetti team. I don't think I'm on his Christmas card list."

"Big deal," Rick replied. "Holloway's a good data engineer but I think he's a jerk."

"Gentlemen," Allan interrupted. "May we leave the

pit gossip for another day and return to the task at hand? Now, Edward, we'll do the first ten laps as before to warm everything up, and then we'll start with…with…"

I waited for him to finish his sentence, but Allan sat motionless, staring hard over my shoulder into the distance. Then the race car's engine died. I turned around and saw two people climbing out of a silver Toyota SUV.

"Good morning, Sophie!" Allan called, smiling broadly. "And Lady Caroline, at last. Lovely to see you again."

Although she really doesn't like being the center of attention, Caroline's athletic grace, long blonde hair, deep blue eyes, and brilliant smile almost always have that effect. She certainly impressed the group of Italian guys next to us, who froze in their tracks and stood there grinning vacantly as she walked past—until their team manager noticed no one was doing anything and started yelling at them.

There were hugs all around for Allan, Rick, and Herb as they welcomed Caroline and introduced her to Konrad. I impatiently waited for my turn, and then crushed her in a long embrace.

"This is great, Caroline! You look…uh…amazing," I said. She always looked amazing but that was the only word my brain was capable of retrieving at that moment.

"And you're looking kind of skinny, Mr. Stewart," she laughed, stepping back. "Sophie, what are you feeding these boys?"

"Ha! They eat like wolves," Sophie replied. "But Eddie, he is always on his exercise machines and he will not eat his desserts anymore. He is very fussy."

"Actually, I think there's another reason," Rick observed quietly. "You should see him some nights, Caroline. The poor guy just sits there at the kitchen table, staring at your picture, picking at his food, pining away as he writes another love poem, and—"

Caroline slugged her brother hard in the shoulder and he darted behind Herb for protection. I put some distance between them by walking her over to the transporter and showing her around.

"Wow, this is a step up from your old truck and trailer, Eddie. You weren't kidding when you said J.R. was serious."

"This is the tip of the iceberg. There's a second transporter identical to this one and two more race cars back at the shop. But what about you? Your classes shouldn't be finished for another few months."

"They're not. My roommate, Sarah, is emailing me the class notes, and I'm sending in my assignments from here. I'll have to go back for final exams except in my favorite course, Documentary Film and Video Production. I have to do a film for that, so I pitched the idea of filming this Indy 500 project to the university — and they went for it. I even got a small production grant to get started. J.R. loved the idea, so here I am, ready to turn all you guys into movie stars. Come and help me unload my gear."

Caroline opened the rear hatch of the Toyota where I had expected to find her usual hand-held video camera, a tripod, and maybe a couple of small digital cameras. Instead, I helped her unload and open two large stainless-steel cases full of very professional-looking equipment.

"This stuff is worth more than my car, Eddie, and I had to beg and plead with the university to let me sign it out. The shoulder camera records digital high-definition video images at twenty-four frames per second, just like a movie camera. The picture quality is awesome. And these two cute little guys are miniature HD digital video cameras. They're small enough to be mounted on the car as an onboard video system."

"You really want to put these on the race car?" I asked.

"Sure. If we put one minicam on top of the roll bar

above your helmet and the other just in front of the cockpit, we can record what you're doing behind the wheel and see exactly what the car's doing at the same time. I can break a single second down into twenty-four individual frames if you want, so that should help your crew fine tune the car. Plus I'll get some great action shots for my documentary."

Allan and Rick thought this was a terrific idea. Within half an hour we had mounted both mini cameras on the car, and Caroline was already roaming around, shooting with her shoulder camera. We restarted the car, and I pulled on my helmet and buckled in. This time I had two checks to do: radio and video. After completing the standard ten laps as a warm-up, I came into the pit for a check-up, and got my orders on the radio from Allan.

"At last, Edward, you may begin to put your foot down. Today we begin testing the car's performance limits. There's lots of time left before we go back to the States, so don't try and break the lap record. No need to go flat out today. Build up to race speed as you feel comfortable."

"OK, boss. Roll the cameras," I said as I flipped down my visor and went back out, slowly building speed over the first five laps.

Having been around the track several hundred

times, Silverstone held few surprises, so I started to try some slightly different lines through the corners and gradually braked deeper into each one. I could feel the speed building and knew that this was much faster than I had gone in testing.

All too soon, Herb held up a "5 MIN" sign indicating that I had time for only a few more laps before they wanted me to come back in. I decided to lay down a flyer; after all, I owed the guys a real scorching lap time as a reward for all of the work they had put in.

I flashed past the pits and set up for turn 1, Copse Corner, arriving at close to 200 miles per hour before touching the brakes slightly and carving smoothly into the apex of the corner. Then I put on a short burst of full power before the Maggotts-Becketts-Chapel series of turns, straining against the G forces before coming out onto Hangar Straight. Unexpectedly, Allan was on the radio.

"The Fillipetti car is ahead of you. He's just going through Stowe."

He certainly was. It was very unlikely that I'd catch him in the next five minutes, but I did want to find out if I could at least close the gap on an F1 car, despite Brian's warning to stay out of the way.

After locking my inside front wheel for a moment under heavy braking, I was through Stowe and into the next series of corners before braking hard again for a tight left-hander. I noticed that my brake pedal felt different, a touch softer than before. But our cars were closer, and the chase was on. I stayed hard on the throttle down the short straight leading up to Abbey corner, before jumping on the brakes again. This time the brake pedal went straight to the floor.

In that instant I knew two things. My brakes had failed—and I was going to hit something hard.

Chapter 10

A Ten-Cent Part

L ater that evening, the six of us sat silently watching *Fast Eddie Trashes the Race Car*, presented in full high-definition video and surround sound, courtesy of Caroline's video equipment. She even displayed the images from both cameras, side by side in slow motion.

From watching the video, there was no doubt that the front wheels just kept on rolling when the brakes should have locked them up solid. The video continued as the car spun to the right and went off the track sideways, tore off its nose and front wing as it clipped a guardrail, plowed through a gravel trap, and slid across a grass verge before it slammed backwards into a second steel barrier.

"Ouch," was Herb's only comment.

"Good thing you spun it, Eddie," Rick observed.

"That gave you enough room to miss hitting the first barrier head on and scrubbed off some speed before you caught the next one."

Even so, it had been a hard impact. The track safety crew had arrived almost immediately, and I had walked away with nothing worse than a sore shoulder.

"A few corners earlier I'd locked the front brakes for a moment," I said. "After that, I thought the pedal felt a bit soft. Kind of spongy. I'd been pushing it, going after that F1 car, and I just thought that the brakes were hot. It wasn't anything drastic. But when I braked hard for Abbey corner—man, I felt that pedal go straight down to the floor. So I spun the car."

"But what caused the brake pedal to go to the floor in the first place?" asked Konrad.

"It might have happened if the brake fluid had air or vapor in it from a leak or over-heating," Herb suggested. "That would have led to a soft pedal or even no brakes. But there were no leaks on that car, plus the brake fluid we use stays stable at temperatures of over 1,000 degrees, so it couldn't have been too hot. And I always put in new fluid and bleed the brakes before a track session. It's got to be something else."

"I agree with Herb," Allan mused. "This wasn't

caused by heat or poor maintenance. I would suspect a leak somewhere, a big one that would quickly cause the loss of all the brake fluid. And as we have just seen: no brake fluid, no brakes.

Allan picked up the remote and turned off the TV.

"I think we've all had enough for today. Let's just be thankful that Eddie was quick enough to spin the car and avoid injury. As for the cause of all this, there will be time enough tomorrow to get to the bottom of it."

The next day, we worked in two teams and went over the car inch by inch. Rick and Herb started at the front, and Konrad and I worked from the back. There was still a lot of gravel, dirt, and grass on the car from the accident, and some of the smaller parts had been crushed, but we were looking for anything that looked like it might have been out of place before the crash.

An hour into the inspection, I was lying on the floor looking at the underside of the car when I felt a light tap on my shoulder. Konrad was kneeling next to me examining one of the rear brakes. As I looked up, he beckoned to me and put his finger to his lips. Herb and Rick had their backs to us at the front of the car.

I rolled out from underneath the back end and knelt beside him. He pointed to the small bleed screw on top of the right rear brake caliper. I hadn't thought to examine the bleed screw. It was almost too obvious, plus it was something that we always checked before the car went out. There was really only one thing that could go wrong with it, but it was critical. If the bleed screw was left open, brake fluid would squirt out every time the driver pushed the brake pedal. Eventually, none would be left, and there would be no brakes. The bleed screw was a ten-cent part, but it could lead to the destruction of a half-million dollar car.

The moment I pinched the bleed screw between my fingers, I could feel that it was loose. Somehow, it had been left partly open. It would only have taken a handful of hard laps before all of the fluid was gone and the brake pedal went to the floor.

"I do not have as much experience as you with these cars, Eddie," he began slowly, "but I know that what I just found is not right. This could be the cause of the leak and the failure of the brakes, could it not?"

"Yes, it probably is."

"Is it possible that it could have somehow opened up by itself on the track, or after the accident?" he asked.

"I doubt it," I replied. "I've never seen that happen."

Konrad took a deep breath and chose his words carefully.

"Then it must be…I mean, the only explanation is that someone forgot to tighten it. It was left open by mistake."

What he didn't have to say was that the person responsible for making sure that the brakes were checked was Herb.

Chapter 11

Trying Not to Lose

Just then, Herb and Rick joined us at the back of the car. Herb immediately understood what we were looking at. He grasped the bleed screw and easily turned it back and forth.

"No way! This thing's just about ready to fall out! Where's the right rear wheel?"

Rick found it off to the side, flipped it over, and ran his finger around the inside of the wheel.

"It's coated inside with an oily film. I'll bet it's brake fluid," he said.

Herb did the same. "Exactly right. Brake fluid everywhere," he said quietly. "Rick, where's my checklist from yesterday?"

Rick retrieved a clipboard from the transporter and handed it to him. We all read over Herb's shoulder as he ran his finger down the long list of items that he had checked off before I took the car out. And right near the top was a line that read, "Right Rear Caliper Bleed Valve Tight" with a check mark and Herb's initials beside it.

We had our answer. Despite what the checklist said, that valve had not been tight before I went out. Every time I had touched the brake pedal, the brake fluid leaked out inside the wheel and onto the track, lap after lap, until there was none left.

A painful silence followed. I knew that things went wrong on race cars for all kinds of reasons, but up until then our team had never experienced a failure just because someone had forgotten to do his job. Konrad seemed ready to accept this possibility, but not Rick or me. We had worked with Herb for ten years, and we knew better.

Faced with this evidence, some guys would have tried to deny or deflect the responsibility, but Herb simply put the clipboard down and faced us.

"It looks like this one's on me. Man, I am so sorry, Eddie. I was sure that bleed valve was tight, and I initialed it. I just can't explain this."

"Don't try," I said. "You never make mistakes like this. As far as I'm concerned, I'm still keeping an open mind."

"I'm with Eddie," Rick added. "I don't care what the checklist says—there's got to be more to it than this."

"More to what?" Allan asked as he walked into the shop and shook the rain from his coat.

We showed him what we'd found and Allan agreed that the loose valve must indeed be the culprit. He even told us of some similar incidents from his early racing days where a car's brakes had simply disappeared.

"Usually we were able to trace it back to a simple mistake from the crew, but there were also a few times when we never did find the cause. In this business, things sometimes just break, wear out, or fall off. So, as to this being your fault, Herb, we can't be completely certain that's true," Allan said.

"Maybe," Herb replied. "But we can't afford any more mistakes like this. There's too much at stake. So from today on, Allan, here's the deal. I'll do my track checklist and initial it, and then I want Rick to check it over again. Same goes for my work in the shop. Double checks for everything I do. We do that or I'm done, and I'll be on a plane home tomorrow. You guys OK with that?"

It didn't look to me like any of us were OK with that at all, but those were Herb's terms. We knew he meant it, and we couldn't afford to lose him. The level of respect I had for Herb before that just went up another notch.

Working under this new arrangement changed things immediately—and not for the better. Each task took longer as everything Herb did had to be double-checked by Rick. But what worried me more than the extra time was the atmosphere in the workshop. Before the accident, we had worked together with the confidence, energy, and easy laughter that came from years of trusting each other. Now, almost overnight, that sense of comfortable camaraderie seemed to have just evaporated. All of us went about our tasks over-shadowed by the lingering fear of another failure. We were no longer working to win. We were just trying not to lose.

It took the rest of the week to repair the crash damage, and time was getting short. Allan wanted a final week of race testing before we packed everything up for our move to Indianapolis. Rick had been having trouble getting access to some of his files on our computer network, so Konrad had driven down to London to sort that out. Then Konrad went on to France to get the latest software updates for the engines.

It was a warm and brilliantly sunny spring day. I was in and out of the pits constantly during the morning as our repairs and setup were double-checked. Sophie brought us lunch and then went with Caroline to set up the video equipment. I wolfed down my sandwich and climbed back in the car.

"All right Edward, I think we're back to where we were before the accident. So, build it up to race speed and start pushing."

"OK."

I snapped down my visor and lit up the rear tires as I left the pits and accelerated hard onto the track. I had waited impatiently for almost a week while the car was repaired and every part checked over twice, so I wasn't worried about another mechanical failure. The track was clear and it was time for me to find out what this car really had. I took three laps to build up to speed and then keyed the radio.

"Allan?"

"Go ahead."

"Can you give me some times this session?"

"OK. Every time you pass the pits, I'll radio you the last lap time."

"Thanks."

For Indy, I'd have a display on my steering wheel to show me the lap times automatically, but for testing we relied on the radio. The fastest machines around Silverstone were Formula 1 cars, and even the slowest of them could easily do a lap time in the 1:26 range. Although our Indy car was heavier and designed to a different set of rules, it had similar power and aero-dynamics. I felt that if we could get close to the F1 level of performance, we would have a good race car anywhere. And maybe something for the guys to smile about again.

The track was clear, and the car was strong and stable as I built up to speed, carving the corners, riding the curbs, braking late, and gradually working it up to the limit.

"1:27.6 last lap. 27.6," Allan radioed.

Not bad. Over the next eight laps I worked that down to a 1:24.8, and there was still some more to come. The EuroTech engine delivered a relentless wave of 800 horsepower, and I was finding a smooth, fast rhythm. I focused hard on carrying a lot of speed onto Hangar Straight and then holding onto it for as long as possible before braking for the sharp right-hand corner at Stowe.

The car turned in smoothly at first, and then I felt the steering wheel jerk and recoil as the left front tire exploded. With an instant loss of grip, the car skated across the corner and speared itself hard into the barrier.

All I remembered after that was the strange, sudden quiet and the searing pain rising up through my left leg.

Chapter 12

Outrageous Fortune

"Caroline have I ever told you…? Your nose…it's just the best," I croaked. Something was wrong with my voice. And my head. It hurt to open my eyes. But looking at Caroline's nose made it worth the effort.

Caroline bit her lower lip and turned away—trying not to laugh, I imagined. But it was true. Her nose was fabulous.

"Here you go. Drink," she ordered as she placed a straw in my mouth.

I hadn't realized how thirsty I was. As I drained the plastic water bottle, I noticed that I had more company. James, Kevin, and Nigel, my three ex-commando fitness trainers from Kent, were standing at the end of my bed. Groggy and confused, I cleared my throat and put down the empty water bottle.

"Kevin, are we running today? Is Caroline coming?"

"No, Eddie. No running for you today," he replied as he pulled up a chair next to the bed. "Caroline's been here with you for the last two nights. We're not at Apex. Allan's just down the hall talking on the phone, and the lads and I arrived this morning. It's good to see you again."

It was good to see them too, especially now that I knew we weren't running, but I couldn't figure out why all four of them were in my bedroom. Unless this wasn't my bedroom. I was starting to feel less groggy as Caroline sat on the edge of the bed and held my hand. She had fabulous hands.

"Eddie, you're in the Horton General Hospital in Banbury," she said gently. "Do you know how you got here?"

I started to shake my head but stopped immediately. It made the room spin.

"I don't think so. I remember that I was testing the car, and then I think I went off, but that's about it."

I tried to push myself into a more upright position. Instantly, I felt a sharp stab of pain in my left leg that cleared my head and brought me fully awake. I pulled back the bed sheet and looked at the bright new plaster cast that ran from just below my knee right down to my toes.

"You've been here for two days, and as you can see, you broke your leg," Caroline said.

Two days in the hospital, a broken leg, and no memory of any of it. The room started to spin again so I decided to fix my gaze on something close and solid. I picked a tattoo on Kevin's forearm. It featured a sword with wings on either side of it and three words underneath that I couldn't quite read.

"Cool tattoo, Kevin," I said. "What's it say?"

Kevin raised his arm so that I could see it clearly.

"It's the Apex motto, Eddie," he said. "It says 'Who Dares, Wins.' That's King Arthur's sword, Excalibur, above it."

"I'll try to remember that. Say, Kevin, I think I'd like to talk to Allan now," I said, closing my eyes.

The Apex guys slipped out as silently as cats, and I sat there quietly with Caroline until Allan came in.

"Well, there you are, Edward! How are you feeling?" Allan flashed his best smile, but it was forced. Underneath it, I could sense his relief and concern. I'd had my share of wrecks in race cars before, but this was the first time that I hadn't been able to remember every detail or to walk away.

"I'm still kind of out of it, but I'm awake now—at least I think I am. I have no clue how I got here or why the Apex guys showed up. But all I want to know right now is what happened to my leg."

"You had an accident at Silverstone, testing the car," Allan replied carefully. "A big one, I'm afraid. The left front tire failed which caused the car to go straight on at Stowe corner. You broke your leg and struck your head on the barrier. You were unconscious when the safety crew arrived, and they had to cut you out of the car. Then it was straight here to the hospital in Banbury and three hours with the surgeon. That was the day before yesterday. I spoke with the surgeon this morning and the good news is that everything went very well. Besides the broken leg, you also have a mild concussion. And he did say that you might have some problems getting through the metal detectors in airports in the future."

"No kidding. Why is that?"

"You had a clean break below the knee that he said would heal up nicely. But there were also quite a few small fractures in your left ankle which required them to use metal plates and screws to piece everything back together. It will all be fine in time, but that cast has to stay on for at least six weeks."

I watched him force another smile and Caroline did the same. They were trying hard to be positive but it was clear to me that neither had had much sleep in the last forty-eight hours.

"Allan, please tell me that the Apex guys were really here. Kevin, James, and Nigel?" I asked.

"Yes, they were. J.R. and I brought them in yesterday. I'll explain that later."

"OK. Caroline, what day is it?"

"Thursday. All day."

"Sorry, I meant the date."

"March 15th."

Almost exactly six weeks to the first day of open practice at the Indianapolis Motor Speedway.

I was discharged from the Banbury hospital by the weekend. Although I was still on some serious pain killers, Sophie had me up every hour, hopping around the house on crutches. It was good to be moving around again, even if it was awkward.

After dinner that first evening, I lunged into the living room and fell into a chair next to the fireplace. Konrad followed and looked around anxiously before he lowered his voice to a whisper.

"Eddie, I am very sorry to see you injured. I was away when you crashed, but when I heard about it I felt terrible. I am worried about you. As a driver, do you not wonder about these accidents? Do you sometimes feel afraid? For a team of this much experience, it seems very strange that such accidents could happen. First the brakes fail, and then a tire explodes. It almost seems that we are destined to fail. It is... outrageous fortune."

That was an expression that I hadn't heard since high school English class. Konrad was right, and it exactly described our situation. Cruel luck—or outrageous fortune—seemed to be stalking our team. None of us was perfect, but with our talent and experience I couldn't accept that these two accidents were simply dumb mistakes. Brakes and tires can fail, but I was seriously starting to wonder if other forces were working against us. There was something new and dark in the back of my mind: fear about what might happen the next time I strapped myself into the car. I tried to shake it off.

"This sport is dangerous and people can get hurt, Konrad," I insisted. "Bad things happen sometimes, even to the best teams. It's no one's fault. It's just racing."

Before Konrad could reply, Allan called everyone into the living room for a team meeting. With the addition of the Apex guys, it was a large group.

"Now everyone, first item: have we all signed Edward's cast?" Allan asked.

"I have not," said Konrad. "I just returned from France this afternoon."

"I'm sure he can find you a space. Now, as Edward has lost most of the last few days, let's get him caught up with what we know about the accident."

"OK. It was a big hit, Eddie, but I guess you know that better than anyone else," Herb said. "There's not much left of the nose section or front suspension. The main tub is a write-off, but it did take on most of the impact and protected you from the worst of it. We'll be able to salvage the engine, gearbox, and rear suspension, but that's about all."

"So we're down to two cars," I said.

"For the moment," Allan replied. "J.R. will get what we need to get us back to three."

"I don't recall the accident itself," I said. "But I do remember the left front tire exploding just before it happened."

"Exactly," Herb replied. "That's what caused it. But we still need to figure out why that tire came apart the way it did. I'll let Rick and Caroline tell you about that."

Caroline jumped in first. "After the accident Rick and I went through the onboard video, frame by frame. We lost both of the minicams in the crash but captured what happened to the tire."

"I'd like to see that video, Rick," I said.

"No, you wouldn't," he replied quickly. "At least

not right now. Maybe I'll give you a copy of it next Christmas. Anyway here's the thing. Tires can pick up a puncture and go down fast, but you would have felt that right away and had some time to react. This one didn't do that. It just blew apart. One second, it's fine and the next—bam! It's in pieces. Incredible!"

"Indeed," Allan added. "I've watched that ten seconds of video a dozen times, and I've never seen anything quite like it."

"But we have," Kevin said quietly.

Everyone's attention turned to Kevin, James, and Nigel at the end of the room.

"Caroline emailed her video footage to J.R. the morning following the crash, and after he had watched it, he forwarded it on to us," Kevin said. "That's why we're here."

"Kevin, you said you had seen this before? Seen what?" I asked.

"We have seen this sort of damage, just not on a racing car. Let's leave it at that for now," he replied evenly.

Chapter 13

The Prince

Allan announced that we would start packing everything up for our flights to Indianapolis the next day, and the meeting broke up. Kevin informed me that I had become shockingly thin and pale from spending too much time indoors, and he insisted that I join him for a stroll around the large garden behind the house. He walked while I hobbled along on my crutches, but there was more on my mind than fresh air.

"So Kevin, are you guys planning on sticking around a while?" I asked.

"We are, Eddie. Actually, J.R. has officially added us to your pit crew. I'll have to practice my tire changing," he replied.

I knew that at some point we were going to need at least three more guys in addition to Herb, Rick, and

Konrad for our pit crew at Indy to refuel the car and change tires during the race. There were often experienced crew men looking to sign on with a team at Indy for the month of May. I had expected that J.R. would hire some of them once we arrived. These jobs were now taken care of, and although they had no racing experience, the Apex guys were smart, tough, and capable. They'd learn fast.

"That's excellent," I said. "It's great to have the three of you around, and I know you've done work for J.R. in the past. But I have a feeling there was more to those other assignments than jogging around the countryside with his executives."

Kevin smiled as we came to a bench and sat down.

"We enjoy the training, but we do have some other skills that aren't listed in the Apex brochure. J.R. didn't bring us in for our expert knowledge of Indy cars, of course. After two suspicious accidents and watching that video of the tire failure, he's concerned."

"I don't know what happened to that tire Kevin, but the first crash was supposedly caused by brake failure. Looks like Herb left a bleed screw open."

"You don't sound convinced," he said.

"No, I'm not really. That's just not Herb. But this second accident had nothing to do with us. Racing tires can fail, but I can't imagine someone making that happen on purpose. It's bizarre."

"I agree. But if we do find that it was deliberate, then I'd take it as a warning."

"What kind of warning?"

"That there's more to come. Got any enemies, Eddie? I mean dangerous ones?"

I thought that over for a minute. I didn't owe anyone money and I didn't possess any top secret information. I'd beaten guys on the racetrack who didn't like to lose but I couldn't see any of them doing something like this. Except maybe one. Raul DaSilva. While I knew DaSilva as a ruthless competitor, he was basically a weasel with money. I expected that he would be dealing with his suspension by partying on his private yacht with his millionaire friends and be back in a year. Then I thought about DaSilva's ex-engineer, Brian Holloway.

"What if there is someone who seems to be convinced that I'm to blame when bad things happen to him? Would that count?" I asked.

I told Kevin about Brian and his warning to me before the accident.

"Brian's basically a hot head," I explained. "And a bully. But I don't see him as someone dangerous."

Kevin wasn't as certain.

"Maybe," he replied. "But we need to pay attention to anyone who might think they have a score to settle with you. If you see him again, be careful."

"OK, Kevin. But honestly, I can't think of anyone else who might be out to get me."

"Good. Now, I will tell you privately that J.R. Reynolds does have an enemy—the truly dangerous kind. And one way to get to J.R. would be to harm those close to him, such as you and your teammates."

"What's J.R. done to make someone want to do that?"

"DynaSport is a very successful company, Eddie, and J.R. is worth a great deal of money, which can attract people who want to get their hands on it. Two years ago, someone hacked into DynaSport's computer system and went after the bank accounts. J.R. brought in a specialist to sort it out, but it went badly. Eventually Nigel had to get involved."

"Nigel? What did he do—chase him around the countryside?" I joked.

"Our Nigel is a man of many talents," Kevin said. "Besides being a cracker-jack commando, he speaks five languages. And he's also an expert in cyber warfare."

"I think I played that once on my computer," I said.

"It's no computer game. Military conflicts these

days are often won and lost on digital information. If you can corrupt or destroy your enemy's information system, orders don't get through, supplies get lost, commanders can't communicate, and planes don't fly. Nige knows all the tricks."

"What's cyber warfare got to do with DynaSport's computer system?"

"J.R. hired a network security expert from Germany named Robert Kruegger to help deal with some aggressive outside hackers, and he did a pretty good job of protecting their system. At least, so it seemed. Within a few months, however, DynaSport's tech director suspected someone was trying to change their financial data, this time from the inside. J.R. called us and we sent Nigel over. He worked under-cover and discovered that the clever Mr. Kruegger had placed a hidden program on the system—a Trojan Horse. It launched itself at night and silently transferred money into a hidden account that only Kruegger had access to. He was getting close to half a million dollars before Nigel discovered what he was up to. The FBI arrested Kruegger and found links between him and similar schemes in Canada and Hungary. He was convicted and sentenced to ten years in prison."

"OK, so why wasn't that a happy ending?" I asked.

"Kruegger escaped on the way to prison. The police transfer van was attacked by a group of gunmen, and the two guards were shot and wounded. It was a professional operation, but Kruegger was also wounded in the exchange of gunfire. Even so, his friends dragged him off and he got away. A month later, J.R. received two long emails signed by someone named 'The Prince' swearing revenge for what had happened to Robert Kruegger. We traced them back to an internet café in Hungary and alerted the Budapest police but the investigation went nowhere. As I said, that was almost two years ago and we haven't heard anything more from 'The Prince.' Until yesterday, when J.R. got this in the mail."

Kevin pulled a folded sheet of paper from his pocket and handed it to me. Someone had neatly typed a simple message:

How all occasions do inform against me, And spur my dull revenge.

> *The Prince*

"We're not exactly sure what to make of it, Eddie," Kevin said. "Why are you smiling?"

"It's Shakespeare," I said with satisfaction. "From *Hamlet* ."

"You think so?" Kevin asked.

"I know so," I replied. "*Hamlet* is one of the greatest

plays ever written and it's all about revenge. I wrote an essay on it and I remember that quote. And Hamlet was a prince. There's another link."

"It's been a while since I read Shakespeare but I remember Prince Hamlet's father is murdered," Kevin said.

"Right," I replied. "He's poisoned and dies, but then his ghost appears to Hamlet and tells him that the murderer was his own brother—"

"Claudius!" said Kevin grinning. "And before Hamlet can do anything, his mother gets remarried to none other than Uncle Claudius, his father's murderer."

"Correct. Then Hamlet loses it and swears to avenge his father's murder," I replied.

"And in the end Hamlet does get Claudius," Kevin continued. "He avenges his father's death, but then he dies as well. So, no one wins. Perhaps that's why I joined the military. The answers are usually clearer."

"Well, this message is pretty clear to me, and it might lead to an answer," I said. "Whoever 'The Prince' is, he's chosen this quote on purpose. Perhaps he sees himself as an avenging hero who must right a terrible evil."

"It's a code of honor," Kevin mused. "He can't rest until he settles the score."

"Exactly. Do you think 'The Prince' is really Robert

Kruegger?" I asked.

Kevin shrugged. "Could be. He clearly has powerful friends and we think he's still out there, waiting for a chance to get back at J.R. Reynolds. One way to do that is to go after what J.R. really cares about, like the people on his race team. And these accidents are getting too close to that possibility for my liking."

After his wife, Susan, the most important people to J.R. are those of us on his racing team. The Reynolds have no children of their own, but I knew that they saw all of us as family. If someone wanted to hurt him, causing us harm would definitely do it.

"Who else knows about this?" I asked.

"Until now, just J.R., James, Nigel, and me. And I need you to keep it that way, Eddie. We thought that you should know the background, but we don't want to alarm everyone else at this point. After all, we may be wrong and you simply had a tire blow out at a very bad time."

"Are you going to look into that? I have to know what happened if I'm going to drive that car again," I said.

Kevin smiled and stood as we began to walk back to the house.

"Most definitely. I've sent the wheel and the video footage off to someone I trust. We'll have some answers soon."

"I knew you three weren't just here to change four tires in fifteen seconds," I said.

Kevin laughed. "Nigel says it can be done in twelve."

Chapter 14

Back-up Plan

April 1st brought no practical jokes my way, but I did get my heavy, itchy plaster cast replaced with a much lighter foam walking cast. It was sort of like a ski boot that I could actually take off for a while.

The break in my leg had healed fairly quickly, but moving my ankle around was painful, even though Sophie made me soak it every night. The doctors in Banbury took a new set of X-rays and confirmed that although my leg was healing nicely, my ankle would take longer. Still, I was ahead of schedule with a real possibility of getting back in the car sooner than expected.

The Indianapolis Motor Speedway didn't officially open for practice until the first of May. That meant we had four weeks to set up shop there and get in some unofficial testing at Chicagoland Speedway, a similar track close by.

The transporters rolled out that night and the rest of us were on an early flight the next morning. I made no new friends in the passenger line-up after my metal ankle plates instantly set off the metal detectors at security, but after I removed the walking cast and showed them the scars, they let me through into the packed Departures area. And right there, I caught a brief glimpse across the terminal of a chubby guy talking rapidly into a cell phone as he handed in his ticket for a flight to Chicago. I wasn't sure, but from behind he looked a lot like Brian Holloway, probably off to his next job.

On the plane, Allan slid into the seat beside me and cleared his throat.

"I truly hope and believe that you'll be ready in a month," he began. "However, the cars are ready now, and we can't have them collecting dust in the shop. There is a lot of setup work to be completed. Actually, we could use another driver."

Allan looked over the top of his reading glasses with a sly smile.

"What would you say to us inviting Stefan Veilleux to join us in Chicago?"

Stefan had won last season in the North American

Formula Atlantic championship where I had finished second. Although we were both fierce competitors, I had become good friends with this small, charismatic French racer. The only drawback I could see was that his English was so bad that we might need an interpreter to understand him.

"Stefan would be a fantastic choice, Allan," I answered enthusiastically. "He's an amazing driver. Not to mention a fun guy to hang out with."

"Then I suggest you check your email when we get to Indianapolis," Allan smiled. "He's just as excited about the idea as you are."

For security reasons, Kevin didn't want us spread out around hotels near the speedway, so he made a few calls and found us another large country house close to Indianapolis for the next two months. This one might not have had the charm of a manor built in 1805, but it had a fully equipped kitchen, the required number of bedrooms, a swimming pool, and all the electronic toys we might need. Kevin especially liked the fact that it came with a brand new, high-tech security system. The only part that he didn't like was that Konrad had plans to spend most of his evenings visiting friends in Indianapolis. Kevin was anxious to keep all of us under one roof as much as possible.

After dropping my gear in my assigned bedroom, I immediately powered up my laptop and checked my email. Sure enough, there was mail from manoftherace@veilleuxracing.com. It was written in his unique version of English.

Hello Eddie!

Yes, this is now Stefan it is who writes email to you. I have not been seeing your face this longs time. How do you go? With me, it is fantastique! I am telling you soon why.

Allan Tanner phones to me. Did you no this? I am very happy. He say that DynaSport has the car for Indy and you are driving her. I am the mazed! Then he say that you are crashed and your leg is bent. I have the sadness for this. But soon you will be not bent so I am again happiness.

But then Eddie, then it is the best! Allan ask me, he say Stefan, do you want testing the car until Eddie is OK. What do I say? I say oui! Yes! I am thrill into the pieces to do this for Eddie who is my friend and for me also Stefan, the man of the race.

So, I am to be coming to Indy the very soonest! I will phones to you.

Stefan

I laughed out loud as I read Stefan's email. Once we put some "booster" padding in the seat, I had no doubt that he would get the most out of our race car.

Did he ever. By the end of Stefan's first hour on the 1.5-mile Chicagoland Speedway oval, he was up to 215 miles per hour and lapping in the 24-second range. Although the track was a few hundred miles from Indianapolis, Allan liked it as we could run the car continuously at over 200 miles per hour and really work on the high-speed aerodynamics.

Stefan loved the smooth power of the EuroTech engine, and the aero package Rick had designed kept the car solidly planted into the fast groove lap after lap. It was a very different experience for me to watch my car blasting around from our pit area with Allan. I hadn't realized how busy he was, tracking and analyzing each lap, talking to Rick, providing quick updates, and making notes to discuss later with his driver.

By the end of that first week of testing, Stefan had completed over 200 laps. And Rick was polishing his glasses more frequently again.

"OK, Wing Commander. You're going to wear out those lenses. What's up?" I asked.

"Nothing to do with the car, Eddie," Rick replied. "It's running great, and Stefan is just reeling off the laps. Man, he's fast."

"Well, the guy can drive, Rick. Trust me, I know."

"Yes, he can," Rick replied thoughtfully. "Look Eddie, here's the deal. We've replaced the crashed car from Silverstone so we're back up to three solid race cars—and two fast drivers. Now that is a good problem to have."

It was, and I knew where Rick's thinking was going.

"So, instead of us just trying to qualify my car, why wouldn't we put Stefan into the spare and try to get him in as well?" I said. "Put two cars in the race. Right?"

"Exactly! Assuming your leg is good to go, J.R. would have two shots at qualifying for the race instead of just one. And if we get both of you guys in the show, J.R. would have a *team* in the 500 rather than just a single car. It wouldn't cost much more to run a second car, and it's way better exposure for DynaSport."

Rick and I went through the details until we felt ready to pitch the idea to Allan. As it turned out, he was one step ahead of us again. In fact, he had already discussed the idea with J.R.

"You two are going to put me out of a job one day if I'm not careful," he laughed. "In any event, you're right. It makes sense. But on one condition."

"What's that?" I asked.

"That you, Edward, will remain our number one driver. J.R. and I are both firm about that. You will be the focus, and we will be doing everything we can to get you qualified. Stefan will have the second car, and while it will be prepared the same as yours, he brings his own crew and he runs his own race. The third car we keep as a spare reserved for you."

During the long drive back to our shop in Indianapolis, Allan explained the deal to Stefan, slowly and carefully, in the back of the truck cab. Stefan listened with growing excitement as he grasped what Allan was offering.

"Oui, yes, but of course, Allan! I am to driving as the second car. Do I care for this? Oui! Yes—I loves to be the team by Eedie! T'ree cars we are having. And Eedie, he is the first. I drives my car the second only. And, if Eedie need the t'ird car, it is his!"

Chapter 15

My Left Foot

It was the right decision for the team, and I respected the loyalty Allan and J.R. had shown to me in the way they handled it. Faced with an injured driver who might not qualify their car at all, some team managers or car owners might have just cut me loose and brought in someone else. Not those two. Instead, they stuck by me as their lead driver, bad leg and all. As soon as I was able, I planned to prove to them that they had made the right decision.

The news that Stefan was officially coming on board as our second driver was greeted with real satisfaction by everyone. Although Konrad had never met Stefan, they appeared to get along well as they chattered away back at the shop in French. I hadn't realized that Konrad spoke French, but since he was working for EuroTech, it made sense. He had some new software updates for the engines that he and Rick were working on, and they were keen to see what kind of mileage our car was getting as we prepared for our final tests at Chicagoland.

We made a new seat for Stefan's car to compensate for his smaller size and painted the car a deep candy-apple red. Meanwhile Caroline prepared the official Indianapolis entries for the two of us. After we dropped them off, I drove her to the airport to catch her flight back to university in California, armed with a brand new pair of replacement minicams, courtesy of J.R. Reynolds.

"It's just a couple of weeks. I'll be back as soon as my exams are finished," Caroline assured me, as I reluctantly let go of her hand. "Take care of that ankle, Eddie."

Allan still wanted to see how the cars behaved in traffic at high speed, and to do that we needed to run them both at the same time. He had hired an extra driver, Mark Davidson, to run laps with Stefan and give my injury a chance to heal.

My leg was feeling stronger every day, however, and I was anxious to get back behind the wheel. J.R.'s people set me up with a local doctor who specialized in sports injuries. After taking a new set of X-rays, we discussed the idea of making up a small brace that would allow me to drive the car while still protecting my ankle. I was lucky that it was my left foot, as all I really needed it for at Indianapolis was to work the clutch pedal during pit stops. Once I had the car up to top speed in sixth gear, all the pressure would be on my right foot to hold the throttle wide open and keep it there.

The doctor finally approved a lightweight ankle brace—but it came with a stern warning not to push too hard as there was a real danger that I could re-injure my ankle. I still had to wear the walking cast most of the time, but I managed to put some break-in miles on the new brace by walking laps around our country house over the next few days. It felt so good that I had to show it off. I propped my left foot up on the table at our regular morning team meeting.

"Check it out, boys. Stretchy fabric, high-top laces, and molded plastic custom-made for my ankle. I just pull it on like a boot and lace it up," I demonstrated. "It really supports the ankle but gives me enough movement to work the clutch."

"Thank you, Edward, for a truly riveting display of footwear," Allan said dryly as he lifted my foot off the table.

Rick fanned the air. "And you might want to wash that thing before it walks out of here on its own."

Allan had Mark start out slowly on the first morning, insisting that he follow Stefan around the huge oval as they gradually built up to speed. Every thirty laps, Allan brought them both in for Konrad and Rick to check the engines and measure their fuel consumption. At the same time, Herb was using the spare car to rehearse our two pit crews.

Fast pit stops were going to be critically important. The rules allowed only six crewmen over the short pit wall to actually work on the car, and each of the six pit stops we planned to make at Indy had to be done perfectly and very quickly—in fifteen seconds or less. Stefan's crew hadn't yet arrived from France, but mine was already practicing. I would have Konrad on the air jack, raising the car off the ground; Rick on the fuel hose; J.R. passing tires; Kevin, James, Nigel, and Herb changing them; and Sophie standing ready with the fire extinguisher. Allan, meanwhile, watched it all and decided when I could go back out. They were simply walking through it step by step at this point. But once we got to Indy, the crews would practice full speed every day, and the stopwatch would be out.

As the morning went on and I watched Mark out on the track in my white race car following Stefan's red one, I grew impatient. I'd been on the sidelines way too long, and I needed to get strapped into the car again. I needed to feel the familiar adrenaline rush of acceleration and pure speed. But desire wasn't enough, and neither was my new ankle brace. There was one key ingredient that I was missing.

Confidence.

Allan finally let me out for a run with Stefan at the end of the day, and I started to feel better about the car. It tracked around the Chicagoland oval as if it was on rails. It was fast, smooth, and stable through the air, both on its own and beside Stefan—even when I was tucked up tight right underneath his rear wing. As I grew more comfortable, I found that the speed came easily. For the first time, I truly appreciated all of Rick's aero and wind tunnel work in England.

As we came into the pit area, shut down the engines, and climbed out of our cars, I noticed J.R. beaming at the two of us.

"I decided to get out of the office and come up here to check things out. Not a bad day's work," he said, holding up a printout of our lap times.

Stefan wiped his face with a wet towel and began rubbing the back of his neck. *Welcome to the wonderful world of G forces, buddy*, I thought ruefully.

"This car, J.R., she loves the speed," Stefan said. "And even if I am to push hard, Eedie he is there always. We are so fast!"

"You've got that right, Stefan," J.R. replied. "Over the last ten laps, both of you were nose-to-tail at 215 miles per hour. How's the ankle, Eddie?"

"Excellent. Didn't notice it at all," I replied.

"Well, get some ice on it right away, just the same. You need to be ready to go tomorrow."

For the final day of the test, Konrad made some adjustments to the engine software and also added the updates to Rick's laptop for the first time. Now that Konrad had granted Rick access to the secrets of EuroTech's software, they constantly had their heads together. Rick was fascinated with the information it provided, especially about how the cars were using fuel. And for 500 miles at Indianapolis, fuel consumption was just as important as outright speed.

"Look at this, Eddie," Rick said as he pointed out the features of EuroTech's software on his laptop. "Each of our cars has its own onboard computer that figures out the best fuel mixture for the engine hundreds of times every second. And everything is linked together electronically, from the throttle pedal all the way back to the engine. See these two windows? One is the data from Stefan's car and the other is from yours. Konrad's set this up so that we'll get a constant stream of data beamed back from the car to the pits while you guys are on the track. We get instant updates on fuel mileage from your engine so we'll be able to work out our pit stops exactly. There's even a second channel on Konrad's laptop to send commands back to the cars."

"Commands for what?" I asked.

Rick shrugged. "Just about anything you want the onboard computer to do."

I nodded. "What about the fuel mixture?"

"Same idea," Rick replied. "With constant data streams from the cars, we can see precisely how much fuel we've used at any point in the race. That way, we can let you guys know if there's enough for you to dial the mixture up to full rich and go for it."

Later, as Sophie served up lunch, I sat down next to Konrad, who picked at his food silently and stared into the distance. He had been working a lot of late nights to get the software right, and he was exhausted. He looked like he could use some encouragement.

"Listen Konrad, you're doing a great job with the software and the engines. Everyone thinks so. The whole package will be perfect for Indy," I said.

"Thank you, Eddie," he said as he smiled thinly. "I just hope everything keeps working well. There is a lot of pressure from EuroTech to see the engines succeed. If something else goes wrong, well, I will lose my job."

"You can't be blamed for the accidents at Silverstone," I said. "Bad brakes and exploding tires have nothing to do with the engines."

Konrad looked around anxiously and lowered his voice.

"Yes, I know, but if something happens with my engines…"

"Look Konrad, we've just had a run of rotten luck up to now. It won't last. It can't. We'll work through it. But not before we've had Sophie's lasagna."

"Thank you, Eddie, but I must excuse myself. I'm sorry, my stomach…" he apologized as he left the table and quickly went into the motor home.

Rick sat down next to me and watched him leave.

"That guy is wound up way too tight, Eddie," he said. "He's a solid engineer and he's worked hard for us, but maybe he's just not cut out for this sport. The stress is really getting to him. EuroTech's on his case every day and the crashes shook him up. He works halfway through the night on the software, and he's always popping those pills. He says they're for his stomach, but I don't know. I'm starting to wonder if he's on something."

That thought was interrupted by J.R. telling me that

I would be driving in the afternoon session. One bite into my lasagna, I realized that I'd left my ankle brace back at my motel room after washing it in the sink and hanging it on the shower bar to dry. Reluctantly, I left my lasagna and borrowed J.R.'s rental car. I got to the motel in record time, retrieved the brace, and was on my way back to the track when the car died. After all of the discussions about fuel that morning, I should have thought to check. It was out of gas.

Chapter 16

Risky Business

I sat in the dead rental car with my cell phone, deciding who to call first. I called local information, got the numbers of three towing companies, and finally connected with the last one. They told me a tow truck would be there in about twenty minutes with some gas. My second call was to Allan to tell him I'd be late, but I just got his answering service. Things got stranger as I placed calls to Rick, Herb, Caroline, and everyone else, but none of them answered.

The truck driver arrived with five gallons of gas and I was on my way. As I parked the car in the pit area, my rumbling stomach reminded me that I'd missed lunch.

As it turned out, I'd missed much more than that.

My first clue was that no one was around and

Stefan's red car was gone. I figured that since I'd been away for well over an hour, they must have decided to send Stefan out to continue testing. I walked out of the pit area and up a few rows in the grandstand to get a better view, expecting to see and hear his red car howling around the speedway. The track was strangely quiet but it wasn't empty. Turn 1 was full of emergency trucks, track officials, and safety workers.

Then I saw Stefan's car, or more correctly, the pieces of it. There was an ugly black impact mark where it had smashed into the concrete wall, and the track was littered with bits of black metal and red bodywork. The force of the impact had carried the car over the top of the wall and into the steel mesh catch-fencing. A thick support pole had shorn it in two. The main tub containing the driver was still in one piece, but the engine and back of the car was a twisted ball of metal farther down the track.

I hobbled back to the rental car, drove it through the pit lane, and raced over to turn 1 as the ambulance pulled away. Everyone from our team was scattered around the accident scene, including the one person I wanted to see the most. Stefan. He was walking slowly toward one of the safety trucks with Rick and Herb, who had their arms around his shoulders. Konrad was carefully collecting pieces of the wreckage.

"Incredible," Allan said, shaking his head.

"How did Stefan walk away from this?" I asked.

"Stefan wasn't in his car," Allan replied. "Poor Mark was. He wanted to compare the setup on Stefan's car to yours, so I agreed to let him take it out while we were waiting for you. Perhaps he just wanted one last run before you and Stefan went out for the afternoon. We may never know."

Mark Davidson was unconscious in the Ann Arbor hospital. It was a long, silent trip home to Indianapolis that night. No one wanted to say it, but we were all thinking the same thing. Our whole Indy project seemed doomed to failure. I had hoped that getting back to the States might change our fortunes for the better. However, every time we seemed to have things going in the right direction, some new disaster slammed us back down.

The only bright spot in the day was that Caroline had finished her final exams early. To celebrate her return, I had arranged to take her out for a fabulous dinner after picking her up at the airport. I'd even polished up my walking cast and bought a new suit and a dozen roses. But, as I was getting ready to go, James politely insisted on accompanying me "for security reasons." Given all the circumstances, my

planned celebration didn't seem appropriate anymore, so we settled for take-out back at the shop with
the guys. So much for Mr. Romance.

This latest blow to the team weighed heavily upon
the shoulders of J.R. Reynolds, who looked pale,
drained, and frustrated as he met with us the following morning.

"I've just got off the phone with Mark's parents and
they're on their way over from England. His left arm,
lower back, and pelvis are broken, but thankfully
there's no spinal cord damage. And, early this morning, he finally regained consciousness, so that's more
good news. I was there when he woke up. I'm going
back up to the hospital in Ann Arbor this afternoon.
But before I do, it's time to clear the air."

He looked around at the still, silent faces.

"Mark says that the car's throttle jammed wide
open going into turn 1. He couldn't stop it. Now, this
is a risky business we're in, and we've all had far too
many reminders of what can happen when things go
wrong. I know the anxiety you feel. Believe me, I can
almost taste it here in this room. I've got some serious
concerns, but it's not about wrecked race cars. Those I
can replace. When people on my team get hurt for
reasons that no one can explain, that's a level of risk
I'm finding very hard to accept. I don't understand

this latest crash but maybe Konrad does. I'd like you to hear what he found."

Konrad took a deep breath, and spoke in a hesitant, nervous voice.

"There is so much damage...such violence.... Forgive me. I have never seen a crash up close before. I can't tell for sure yet, but Mark's accident may have been caused by a failure of the engine's computer program. The throttle would not release from full power. This...this is unheard of. No EuroTech engine has ever failed in this manner. And there is something else...the software was changed somehow. I'm still checking, but that could have caused the throttle to stick wide open."

"I want an answer, Konrad," J.R. said. "Find the problem and find the source. Do whatever it takes."

Our four days of testing had painfully convinced Stefan that he wasn't going to last 500 miles in an Indy car without some serious work, so early the following morning Allan, Herb, and I dropped him off at a gym before driving to the shop. We arrived to discover two forensic investigators from the Indianapolis police department examining the wreckage from Mark's crash behind bands of yellow police tape.

We looked through the window of the shop office

and saw Konrad slouched over his desk in a deep sleep next to his computer. Evidently, he had been working through the night again. Herb decided that the best thing for Konrad was a jolt of "real coffee," so he left to make a pot. Meanwhile, Allan and I knocked on the door until Konrad finally woke up and let us in.

"Eddie…Allan…what time is it?" he mumbled.

"Just after eight," I replied. "When J.R. told you to keep working on this, Konrad, I don't think he meant around the clock. Man, you look terrible."

Konrad's hands shook as he rubbed his bloodshot eyes and reached for a large bottle of pills. He popped six into his mouth, chewed them quickly, grabbed a water bottle, and washed them down. He looked at us weakly.

"They help my stomach. It has been very bad since we left England," he explained. "I spoke to EuroTech last night after the meeting and…they are furious. They demanded to know what had happened to the engine, so I worked last night with Rick on the software. He left early this morning, but I kept going."

"Any answers?" I asked.

Konrad took a deep breath and ran his fingers through his mottled hair.

"The engine failure at the Chicago track was caused

by corruption in the EuroTech engine software. It had been hacked. I had to go right into the source code and check it line by line. It took all night but I found it. A complete section of code was changed to make the engine instantly accelerate to full power after a certain time. The driver would have no warning of this. And he would have had no way to stop it."

"Couldn't he have just shut the engine down or popped it out of gear?" I asked.

"No," Konrad replied. "Everything is electronically controlled through the car's computer. The software was changed to block out all of the driver controls."

"Who could have done this?" Allan asked.

"This type of reprogramming would have required a computer expert—but I have traced how it was done. In England, I put all of our computers onto a network so that we could share information and work together as we do here. I designed a very secure network, and each of us has access to certain things on it. But the only person who had access to the EuroTech program was me. At least, until the final day of the test when I gave Rick access to the program for the first time so that we could both monitor the cars."

"I remember. He was really impressed with what that program could do," I said.

"It is impressive" he nodded. "EuroTech has spent

millions developing it, and there are people who would like to have that software for themselves. They would pay a great deal of money to get it. Of course, EuroTech guards its secrets carefully. That is why I was assigned to work with your team."

"Let's get to the bottom line. Who was it?" I asked.

I was just waiting for Konrad to drop one of two names: Robert Kruegger or maybe even Brian Holloway. After all, both had the technological know-how and the motive to pull off something like this.

"I traced it back to the final day of the test at Chicago, between the time I granted Rick access to the program and the moment before Mark went out in the car. The network records show who logged in, what was done to the program, and also where the copies of the stolen software code were sent. The person who did this logged in as 'Wingman'."

I knew exactly who 'Wingman' was. Rick Grant had used that login since junior high school.

Chapter 17

Inspector Williams

I punched the door open as I stormed out of the office and limped straight over to our motor home. There, I was amazed to find a strange burly man in a houndstooth jacket drinking coffee with Rick, Herb, Caroline, James, and J.R. All of them were huddled around the dining table, which was covered with papers, cell phones, Caroline's video camera, a laptop, and a scanner.

"Good morning! You must be Eddie," the newcomer said with a wide smile. "I'm Inspector Williams, a former associate of Kevin's. Please join us, although I must warn you about this coffee Herb has made. It's shattering."

"J.R., I need to talk to you right now," I demanded, ignoring the man's reference to Herb's "tar blend" coffee. "I want to know exactly what's going on. Konrad seems to think that Rick's involved with

Mark's crash and I'm not buying that for a second!"

"It's OK, Eddie, we know all about it," J.R. said evenly. "Inspector Williams here has been working with Kevin and me lately. We just received some new information from last night that may answer some of your questions."

"Don't worry, Eddie," Kevin said. "No one suspects Rick of anything. Peter—Inspector Williams, that is—has analyzed the tire from your Silverstone accident. He has also been going over the onboard video of the laps just before the second accident. And he's found some interesting information for us."

"Well, based upon an examination of both the video and the tire," Williams began, "I feel fairly certain now that your flat was actually the result of a marksman's bullet. Someone shot the wheel right out from under you."

I stared at him in stunned silence.

"I specialize in the areas of ballistics, explosives, and high-tech crime at Interpol—the International Police agency," Williams continued. "Kevin forwarded the evidence and the details to me shortly before you left England. Interpol focuses on crimes that overlap our member countries, including England and the United States. It has been quite an intriguing case for us."

"Why is that?" Allan asked.

"I do love a puzzle, and this is an odd one," Williams replied. "Your wheel gave us a good start."

"What did you find?" Kevin asked.

"Usually bullets are made of lead, but these bullet fragments were pure copper, which we usually only see on a hollow point design. That sort of bullet is designed to break apart into fragments on impact which takes out large chunks of anything with a fairly thick hide, usually a heavy, big-game animal. Or, in this case, a racing tire. You can see the fragments clearly in the pictures."

I looked across the table at Allan as he leaned back in his chair looking grim.

"Furthermore, thanks to Miss Grant's excellent video footage, I was able to locate the source of the gunshot. The shooter was sitting in a white van parked by the fence at the edge of the oval."

"We were just able to make out a license plate number on the van right before you hit the barrier," said Kevin. "Peter and the British police traced it back to a local rental agency near Silverstone. The booking was made online using a stolen credit card."

"The shooter left the van back at the rental office the following evening," Williams continued. "It had been thoroughly cleaned, but we did find a very small trace of gunshot residue inside the driver's door frame. That puts our shooter in that van at Silverstone. And even though the interior had been wiped clean, we were able to recover part of a thumbprint from behind the rear view mirror."

"So you've got the right van, but what about who rented it?" Herb asked.

Williams leaned forward with a predatory gleam in his eyes.

"Well, a partial thumbprint isn't much good unless you can match it to a complete print, and we haven't had anything to work with—until now."

"What do you mean, 'until now'?" I asked.

"Here's what's happened in the last few hours," Kevin said. "As I told you earlier, Eddie, our Nigel is quite an expert in computer systems security. He knows all about how to get in and out of computer networks without being discovered. Last night, Nigel quietly hacked his way into our shop network while Konrad and Rick were trying to sort out what had happened to the EuroTech software. Nigel and Peter sat back and watched what they were doing from this laptop here in the motor home until Rick left at four o'clock this morning. Then, Konrad locked the office door and kept on working."

"I know," I replied. "I just finished talking to him.

Someone got into the EuroTech software and replaced part of it with code that caused the engine to run wild at Chicago. Mark never had a chance. Konrad thinks he's traced it back to Rick."

"Well," James said slowly, "perhaps not. Go on, Kev."

"Konrad finally stopped working and passed out at his desk at about seven this morning," Kevin said. "But we know that as soon as Rick left, three hours earlier, Konrad rebooted the system, logged in, and went straight to the hacked lines of program code. He then put back the original code from a very high density CD. We now think that he could easily have done the same thing at Chicago then replaced the altered code later to cover his tracks. When he was finished, he changed the login records to 'Wingman,' which built a trail back to Rick. Then he finally collapsed on the desk from exhaustion. James and I wanted a look at that disc, so we picked the lock and slipped into the office. I don't know if Konrad was in a hurry or if he was just too tired to think straight, but after all those technical tricks and cover-ups, he made one very simple mistake. Well, two mistakes, actually. He forgot to put the disc away. And he didn't handle it very carefully."

James gently picked up a plastic bag containing a

silver disc and rotated it so that we could see both sides. He passed the disc to Williams.

"At the very least, the computer code on this CD tells me that Konrad has some explaining to do," Williams replied. "But there is also a thumbprint here that may tell us much more. After watching Konrad's actions early this morning, I scanned the thumbprint on this disc. Then I had my contacts at Interpol and the Indianapolis police check to see if it came up as a match on their databases. I should have an answer shortly."

"Close enough for me," Herb said as he stood up. "If that print matches up to the one from the van at Silverstone, then Konrad's the guy. Let's just go have a chat with him."

"Hold on, Herb," Williams interrupted. "Konrad doesn't know yet that we suspect him. I want to keep it that way and see what his next move is. He may be the source of the 'The Prince's' threatening letters and the racing accidents, or he may lead us to someone else who is masterminding the whole plot. Nigel's back in the shop, keeping an eye on him along with the investigators from the Indianapolis police. He's not going anywhere, and for now we'll wait to see if his print turns up anything interesting. If it does, then we'll close the net quickly."

From the day he had joined the team back in England, Konrad had been edgy and anxious, but I had accepted that as part of his nature. Even though he'd just been caught in the act of trying to frame Rick for the software failure, I still couldn't picture him as the source of all our trouble. He might have just been trying to save his job.

Unless…

"*Outrageous fortune…*" I muttered to myself. When Konrad first used that phrase after our second accident in England, I knew I'd heard it before. When Williams mentioned the letters, 'The Prince's' quotes from Shakespeare tugged at my memory. Some pieces of the puzzle started to fall into place.

"I think I might have something else," I said. "I once heard Konrad use the phrase 'outrageous fortune' when he was talking to me about all the things that had gone wrong for us. It struck me as an odd thing to say. I knew that phrase but couldn't quite remember why. But now I'm almost sure that it's from—"

"*To be, or not to be,*" Caroline exclaimed in a strong stage voice. "*That is the question; Whether 'tis nobler in the mind to suffer the slings and arrows of outrageous fortune or to take arms against a sea of troubles, and by opposing end them.* Eddie's not the only one who paid attention in English class. That's Hamlet's biggest speech in the play."

"Exactly! And Hamlet was the Prince of Denmark," I added. "And that letter from 'The Prince' was also a quote from Hamlet. Obviously, Konrad Andersen also knows his Shakespeare well enough to quote Hamlet in everyday conversation. I'll bet all the metal in my leg that he used that quote from Hamlet to threaten revenge and then signed it as 'The Prince'."

"But the question here is, revenge for what? The words on this note were carefully chosen. Revenge is a powerful motive that can drive people to do all sorts of terrible things. And like the play, it won't end until someone dies."

That's when we heard two distant shots, and I remembered that I'd left Allan alone in the office with Konrad.

Chapter 18

Out of the Shadows

We burst out of the motor home and ran, or in my case limped frantically, back into the shop. We arrived to find Konrad, pinned face down on the floor, with Nigel's knee in the middle of his back. The office was covered in broken glass, and a small black pistol lay a few feet away from Allan, who sat stunned in one of the office chairs. We watched as two Indianapolis policemen handcuffed Konrad, pulled him to his feet, and marched him out, right past all of us.

No one said a word, but I saw the savage hatred in Konrad's eyes as he stared at J.R. In that moment I knew that I was looking at the source of everything that had gone wrong since the Indy project began. I turned to Inspector Williams beside me.

"Did you see that look?" he asked.

I nodded. "Now that, I believe," I said quietly.

"I thought that I was in one of those reality police shows on late night television," Allan told us the next morning as we finished a team breakfast around the swimming pool.

"As soon as you left the office, Eddie, Konrad started frantically searching for something. He looked everywhere until he finally went over to the drive on the big computer, popped it open, and saw that it was empty. I tried to talk to him but he was becoming frantic. That's when the gun came out, and Nigel... arrived."

In fact, Nigel had launched himself through the office window feet first at full speed. He'd flown over top of the desk and drop-kicked Konrad straight out of his chair. Konrad had managed to get off two wild shots that went into the ceiling on his way down, but Nigel had rolled back onto his feet, kicked the gun from Konrad's hand, and pinned him to the floor just as the Indianapolis police burst through the door. It was all over in a few seconds.

"Brilliant!" Kevin stated with obvious pride. "Perfect timing and a classic surprise entry to strike, roll, and disarm. A thing of beauty, Nige!"

Nigel smiled shyly and shrugged. "It was all right."

Inspector Williams came out of the house, holding a thick file of papers.

"Well, in the last twenty-four hours it's become clear how close some of you were to a very nasty end. The police and I eventually convinced Konrad that he would be wise to cooperate, and we've learned a great deal overnight. First of all, Mr. Konrad Andersen is not who he pretended to be. We did match the partial thumbprint from the white van at Silverstone to the complete one on the CD from Konrad's computer. It belongs to a gentleman by the name of Dimitri Ritzlov," Williams said.

"Didn't he play for the Detroit Red Wings?" Herb asked.

"No, I think not," Williams replied. "The Interpol report I have here indicates that Ritzlov is a former Russian KGB intelligence agent. No pictures unfortunately, but quite a lot of information. Ritzlov speaks four languages, has a degree in computer programming, and is an expert in ballistics and explosives. Apparently, he was a gifted actor in his university years as well. The CIA suspects that he was originally planted in the U.S. five years ago to hack into military networks and gain information.

"Ritzlov was very good, but he liked his American luxuries," Williams added. "He had a taste for expensive clothes, fast cars, and high-stakes gambling. So he began to run operations on his own—stealing passwords and gaining access to the bank accounts of large companies. Interpol also thinks he hired himself out to criminal gangs in Russia and Europe."

"That's a pretty good spy story, but why would a guy like Ritzlov be interested in us?" I asked.

"Dimitri Ritzlov, as it turned out, had a younger brother, Sergei. They were working together to steal funds from DynaSport, with Sergei on the inside and Dimitri on the outside. Sergei was using the name of Robert Kruegger at the time."

This was getting complicated in a hurry.

"Wait a second," I said. "So Konrad Andersen is really Dimitri Ritzlov. And Robert Kruegger is really Sergei Ritzlov, his kid brother?"

Williams held up his index finger.

"Sergei was Dmitri's kid brother. Dimitri—that is, Konrad—gave us all of the details last night. Go back to three years ago. Robert Kruegger—Sergei—was arrested but escaped on his way to prison. His brother, Dimitri, organized the escape, but it didn't go as planned. Sergei was shot twice and died of his wounds hours later. Dimitri was devastated. Sergei was fourteen years younger, and Dimitri had always looked after him: he'd put him through school, sent him money, and taught him everything he knew about intelligence, computers, and spyware. They were partners. Dimitri would hack into a company's network from the outside, and then Sergei would go in to fix it."

"And once Dimitri was on the inside, he could get at the big money," J.R. said.

"That's how they operated," Williams said. "They pulled off three other jobs before they got into DynaSport and Sergei was caught. After Sergei died, Dimitri placed the blame squarely on J.R. Reynolds, and he wanted revenge. In Dimitri's mind, J.R. had destroyed Sergei. He wanted J.R. to lose someone close to him, someone he cared for deeply like a younger brother. Someone like you, Eddie. He spent almost two years planning how to do it and yes, he found inspiration in *Hamlet*."

"So how does Konrad—I mean, Dimitri—fit in with the accidents?" Rick asked.

"Dimitri did his research and he was patient. He knew J.R.'s passion for racing and his closeness to Eddie, so he got a job in motor sports with EuroTech. When DynaSport announced the Indianapolis 500 team, Dimitri saw his chance. He convinced EuroTech to contact Allan. Once that deal was done, he arranged to get himself assigned to your team, and he was in."

"Wow," Rick said. "The guy was different, but I just thought he worked late because he wanted to. He was great with the engines, and we trusted him with the cars."

"We certainly did," Allan said. "That's how he was able to get close enough to cripple our efforts."

"Oh yes," Williams nodded. "In fact, he was quite proud of how well he'd deceived you all. His ultimate goal was to avenge his brother's death by killing Eddie in spectacular fashion at the Indianapolis 500. He felt that would even the score, but he wanted to work up to it slowly and watch your team fall apart first. It only took a few moments when Herb's back was turned for him to loosen the brake bleed screw and cause the first crash at Silverstone. He then moved up to something more complicated and shot out the tire that caused the second crash."

"That fits," Rick said. "He said he was away that day, supposedly in France. Instead, he was sitting in that van with a rifle, waiting for Eddie."

"Correct," Williams continued. "In Indianapolis, he corrupted the EuroTech engine software and caused the third crash at the Chicago test. Dimitri set up "Wingman" Rick to take the fall for that crash and get him fired from the team. Then he would be free to prepare his final plan."

"And now I know how he could have done it," Rick said. "He had configured his laptop to receive data from Eddie's car, and he also had a second stream to send commands back to its onboard computer."

"Including a command to a wireless detonator," Kevin added. "Remember that Konrad was an explosives expert."

Stefan's eyes were wide with shock. "A bomb? It was for Eedie?"

"I'm afraid so," Kevin said. "We found and searched an apartment he had rented where we discovered C4 plastic explosive concealed inside a spare engine computer. He planned to switch the engines on the morning of race day. There was more than enough to have blown the front end of the car away and to make sure that Eddie—"

"OK, we get it," Caroline said, taking my hand.

There wasn't much left to say. I stared as the water gently rippled across the surface of the pool and slowly felt the weight of stress and anxiety begin to lift. The truth was awful, but the danger was over. For the first time in months, I felt that I was finally walking out of some long shadows. I turned to Allan and J.R.

"May I please just drive the race car now?"

Allan smiled.

"Yes, Edward. You may."

Chapter 19

Rookie Test

"The Indianapolis 500 is unlike any other race in the world," Allan said as I posed in my race car while Caroline took some new pictures for our website.

He was right. At any other track, we would have arrived on Thursday, practiced on Friday, qualified on Saturday, and raced on Sunday. Not at Indy. Teams arrived on the first day of May and spent the entire month practicing, qualifying, and fine-tuning their cars. The race wouldn't take place until Memorial Day Sunday at the end of the month.

"It's really quite dramatic, Eddie," Caroline agreed. "Imagine this. In Act One, we meet our hero, Fast Eddie Stewart, as he streaks around the Indianapolis Speedway on the way to passing his rookie driver's test. Then it's on to Qualifying. He knows that he needs to set one of the top thirty-three fastest speeds in the qualifying sessions. Otherwise, dashing young

Eddie won't even get a starting spot in the big race. If he succeeds, he moves on to the middle part, or Act Two."

"Could I be handsome and fearless as well as dashing?" I asked.

"Easily," Caroline replied with a wink.

"So, for Edward the Handsome and Fearless, Act Two is all about surviving," Allan continued. "This is a 500-mile race but he must get through the first 400 miles without a mechanical failure, an accident, or a major mistake during a pit stop. If he manages that, then he makes it into the final act—the last 100 miles, where this race is won and lost. The trick is to keep out of trouble while running fast enough to stay on the lead lap going into the final 100 miles."

"And what's the ending, Caroline?" I asked.

"My favourite ending is the one where Fast Eddie wins," said Caroline. "He gets a huge trophy, a big drink of milk, and a really large cheque. Then he sweeps the beautiful Caroline away for a decent dinner."

"But not before he lets her kiss him on worldwide TV," I added.

"We'll see," she replied.

The track officially opened on May 1st, and all of the

teams spent the next week moving into their garages in Gasoline Alley. After Konrad was arrested, Rick had received a personal call from the president of EuroTech, who promised him full control of the engine software and a shipment of new computers for us to use. Rick was in his element setting them up in our new Gasoline Alley garage office. Allan had also found the parts to build up a third spare car to replace the one that had been destroyed in the Chicagoland crash. Meanwhile, I had been cleared by the track medical staff to drive with my ankle brace. Things were definitely coming together nicely for the first week of practice.

I'd driven on large oval tracks before, but none of them even came close to the sheer size of the Indianapolis Motor Speedway. Laid out in 1911, the track is a giant two-and-a-half-mile bowl with two flat straightaways connected by four left-hand corners, each with a gentle nine degrees of banking. A lap at Indy is 2.5 miles, and it only takes 40 seconds to complete at 225 miles per hour. At that speed an Indy driver covers the length of a football field in less than one second.

We prepared for our rookie tests by watching our practice laps on Caroline's video, talking to some of the other drivers who had raced at Indy before, and attending the rookie drivers' meetings. We learned that the Indy rookie test had four parts. Each driver had to put in at least ten consecutive laps starting at a speed of 200-205 miles per hour, then ten more laps at 205-210 miles per hour, then another set of ten at 210-215 miles per hour, and then a final ten laps above 215 miles per hour. Anyone who failed to reach and hold those speeds would not move on to qualifying.

We joined five other rookie drivers on May 8th for our test, and thanks to Rick's aero package, our cars were awesome. Sixty-seven laps later, Stefan topped the rookie speed charts at 221.38 miles per hour and I was right behind him at 220.75 miles per hour. Three more rookies passed but six others didn't. They packed up their garages and left. Our garage area, on the other hand, was full of excitement in anticipation of the first official practice session the following day.

Practice began at noon, but this time there wasn't just a handful of rookies. We were fifty-two cars and drivers entered for thirty-three spots. That meant that there were always at least a dozen cars on the track at any given time. Stefan and I usually went out together, and we were impressed with how well our cars behaved when we were running fast in a tight pack. I also had a chance to follow some of the other cars around, especially Michael Cerelli, who had won the 500 twice, and Ryan Burrell, who had set a new track record in qualifying last year. They were both slowly working their cars up to speed, and I improved my cornering lines by following, watching, and learning from two of the best.

By the second full week of practice I knew that we had two fast cars that could comfortably run in the range of 215-220 miles per hour. If I could hold it together for four qualifying laps, I felt sure we'd nail a starting spot. After everything we'd been through to get here, I didn't want to be one of the cars that failed to make the cut.

We waited until mid-afternoon for the track to cool down to try out our qualifying setup. Stefan's setup seemed to suit him just fine and his run went fairly smoothly. Then it was my turn. Once I'd laid down a few warm-up laps, I ran six more laps flat out at just over 224. Still, I felt that I could have gone a tick faster without the wind, which tended to push the car from side to side on the back straightaway. Between the wind and the heat, one thing I'd learned was that the track surface at Indianapolis was always changing.

Allan brought me back in and we closed up the garage for the day. He seemed satisfied as he sat down with the team. It was good to see him smiling most of the time again.

"Well gentlemen, I believe that we have two cars ready for tomorrow," he said. "The rules require us to use the same engines we had in the cars for qualifying, so I don't want to wear them out. Nothing left to do but wait for tomorrow."

I hate waiting.

Chapter 20

Making the Show

Like most things at Indy, qualifying for the race was different from anywhere else. Day 1 was Pole Day, when the first eleven of the thirty-three available spots were filled and the fastest qualifier would be decided. Eleven drivers' names were drawn from a hat, and each of them was allowed three warm-up laps and then four timed laps, which were averaged to produce a qualifying time.

Once those cars were qualified, then the track was open to anyone else who thought they could "bump" one of them out of the first eleven spots. At the end of Day 1, those top eleven spots were secured and any-one in those eleven spots was in the race. Day 2 filled starting spots twelve to twenty-two in the same manner. When it was over, the next eleven starting spots were secured. It was best to qualify on Day 1 or 2 as your spot in the race was then guaranteed.

But if you weren't fast enough, you had to wait for Day 3 when you faced your last chance to make the field of thirty-three cars. Only eleven spots were left. This final day was often called "Bump Day" as all of the drivers who hadn't yet secured a starting spot frantically tried to bump someone faster and get one of the final eleven places. The competition was fierce as the names in that last group changed every few minutes. It was great for the fans and provided lots of excitement as drivers fought for the final eleven starting spots.

Or not. It all changed when the first two days of qualifying were rained out. The showers started from a dawn sky the color of lead on the first morning of qualifying, and they didn't let up for the next two days. When the skies finally cleared, we were told that positions 1 to 22 would be decided on Pole Day, and all the rest would be filled the next day, with bumping on both days. The numbers went into the hat and we were all relieved when Stefan drew number 14 in the qualifying line and I drew 19 for the first day. That meant that we had a chance of nailing down a starting spot in the top half of the field.

Up until then, I hadn't really noticed much of a crowd, but now that qualifying had started, they were coming in by the thousands. The first runs were scheduled from noon until six o'clock, and the grandstands started to fill right after sunrise. We spent the morning going over every inch of the cars to make sure that they were all set.

Finally, the first car took to the track—and qualifying was underway. Stefan and I strapped into our cars and Allan gave us updates on the radio. I was surprised at how quickly the line moved.

Just before two o'clock, Stefan pulled out onto the track for his warm-up laps. We knew that the speeds so far ranged from 215 to 227 miles an hour, and that the fastest time had been set by the Brazilian driver Carlos Molina at 227.184. Allan figured that a four-lap average around 223 or 224 would be enough to qualify, and I listened anxiously as he read out the speed after each of Stefan's four timed laps. His first lap came in at 223, then 224, 225, and finally another 224. Officially, Stefan posted a four-lap average of 224.337 which put him in the top six. Five drivers went ahead of me and none of them went over 221 except Michael Cerelli who posted a stunning four-lap average of 228.194 miles per hour. That would likely put him on the pole as the fastest qualifier.

Finally, it was my turn, and as they waved me out, I carefully brought the car up to speed over my three warm-up laps. The track was fast and the car felt smooth and strong as I carved through turns 1 and 2 on the first of my four timed laps. I could feel the speed building as I flashed across the finish line to complete the opening lap. On the back straight again for lap 2, I glanced down at my steering wheel display and saw a speed of 224.471 for my first lap. I felt that lap 2 was better—and it was, at 226.320. Lap 3 was amazing at 228.010. I was having a great run and pushing hard on my fourth and final lap when the rear end of the car twitched coming out of turn 3 and I had to lift off the throttle for an instant to regain control. It was more of a wiggle than a serious slide, but I knew that it had cost me some speed. As I crossed the finish line and slowed down, I checked the dash display and saw that my final lap came in at 223.431. I keyed the radio.

"Hey, Allan! How was that?"

"Very nice indeed, Edward! A four-lap average of 225.558. And a 228 on lap 3! You're in the top five right now."

"So, are we in the show?"

"There's still a few hours left, but I think that by six p.m., J.R. can look forward to having two cars in the field."

We spent the remainder of the afternoon glued to

our trackside television monitors watching the rest of qualifying. Although a couple of guys eventually went faster than we did, when it was all over the official results listed #34 *Eddie Stewart* in 7th spot at 225.558 miles per hour, and #35 *Stefan Veilleux* in 10th at 224.337.

We were in the show: we officially had starting spots in the Indianapolis 500. There was a huge celebration back at our garage as all of us felt the stress of the last three months melt away. Sophie went all out and prepared a massive dinner for the team back at the motor home where we all ate too much. Afterward, we sat back and watched Stefan and his crew trying to sing Irish pub songs with Inspector Williams in French. I looked around at the smiles that I'd missed for too long and felt that I'd finally found my way back home.

Now that qualifying was taken care of, our focus could turn to our pit stops. At Indy, pit stops are huge—the race can be won or lost by the work of the pit crews. On race day, we planned to stop every thirty laps for a full load of fuel and new tires. Our two crews had been practicing hard every day once we set up at the track, since each car is only allowed six crew members to do that work perfectly in the space of about fifteen seconds.

Stefan was using the same crew of ace mechanics he had worked with to win the Formula Atlantic championship, and they were fast and efficient. Best of all, they spoke French and were able to communicate with Stefan. By comparison, my crew had never worked together before; but if practice was anything to go by, I felt that they would eventually be as fast as anyone. Caroline had taken over Konrad's former job of jacking up the car with the air hose, and Inspector Peter Williams was thrilled to accept Sophie's invitation to join my crew and man the fire extinguisher.

"It's just like training for a mission," Kevin told me. "We practice how it's supposed to go, but we also prepare for things that can go wrong. We're ready for the normal tire changes on a scheduled pit stop, but we've also practiced how to change a damaged wing, start a stalled car, or put out a fire. You never know, Eddie. Expect the unexpected."

Allan outlined our race strategy to Stefan and me as we sat in the empty grandstands and gazed down the long, front straight.

"Now then, we're going to keep this very simple. First of all, remember that this is a 500-mile race, 200 laps, so do not try to win it in the first 15 minutes, gentlemen. We're starting near the front in seventh and tenth, so we will try to hold those positions, stay with the lead pack, and keep ourselves out of trouble. We'll set a comfortable pace for you and your cars. Never underestimate how physically demanding this race is going to be. This is a marathon—not a sprint."

Carving the turns at over 200 miles per hour meant that I'd be straining against G forces of three to five times my body weight every lap for 500 miles, exposing any weakness in conditioning or my still-tender ankle.

"The EuroTech engines and software will give us good mileage. If we're patient and careful early on," Allan continued, "we should have enough fuel to dial up the mixture and have maximum power over the last forty laps."

Every team started the 500 with the same amount of fuel in their pits, and teams constantly monitored their car's mileage during the race for one simple reason: once your fuel was used up, you stopped. Hopefully that didn't happen until the race was over but if you used too much fuel by going too fast too early, you might not have enough left to make it to the finish. On the other hand if you conserved too much fuel, you would be too slow and fall hopelessly behind. In other words, a rich mixture produced more power and speed but burned more fuel, while a lean mixture saved fuel at the expense of power. The key was to find the right mixture of fuel going into the engine to produce decent power and speed, while making sure you had enough to last 500 miles.

Our cars had a small red dial on the steering wheel that allowed Stefan and me to adjust the fuel mixture while we were driving. It looked just like a volume control knob with positions from one up to ten, and we relied upon Allan and Rick to tell us when to dial it up or down. Positions 1 through 4 saved fuel but dropped our power and speed, while positions 7 through 10 gave us lots of power and speed but burned more fuel. We planned to start the race at position 5 or 6 and then dial the mixture down to save fuel for later in the race. If everything worked out as planned, we would have enough fuel left to run the engines wide open over the last 100 miles when it mattered most.

"But we also need to look after our tires," Allan continued. "We only get six sets for the race, and I'd like to save one for the final stop. If we can manage the fuel and tires, then we should be in very nice shape for the last 100 miles."

Allan smiled at us and folded his arms.

"And then—you go flat out."

Chapter 21

Gentlemen, Start Your Engines!

Race day began for me at five thirty in the morning with three loud thumps on the motor home bedroom door and the appearance of Herb with a mug of "real" coffee.

"Rise and shine, racer boy," he said. "Breakfast is almost ready. And it's going to be a treat!"

Twenty places were set at folding tables when I arrived. On one side of the garage, I saw Stefan's crew cooking paper-thin crêpes, slicing fruit, and whipping up fresh cream. On the other side, Kevin, James, Nigel, and Allan were cooking eggs, sausages, bacon, and potatoes, and making toast. Dueling breakfasts. I decided to keep the peace and took a little from both sides.

After breakfast, the checklists came out for each car. This was our final chance to go over the cars, part by part, before the race began, and we left nothing to chance. By mid-morning the tool chests were packed, the pit carts were ready, and Stefan and I had changed into our driver's suits. Finally, we filled the fuel tanks, Rick uploaded the fuel-mapping software, the engines were fired, and the cars warmed up. We were ready.

Gasoline Alley was now packed solid with crowds of spectators. Overnight, the Speedway had been transformed into a small city as the grandstands swelled with the arrival of 250,000 people, and crowd noise filled the air. At ten thirty, we got the call to push the cars out of the garage, hook them up to our pit carts, and tow them to the pit lane.

The crews rode with their cars and pit carts, but at Indy it's a tradition for the drivers to walk the length of Gasoline Alley out to the pit road. This hasn't changed in fifty years and the fans love it. The track security guards blew their whistles, the crowds part-ed, and off we went. Stefan and I put Caroline between us and we set off, feeling like a trio of rock stars.

There is a series of prerace traditions leading up to the Indianapolis 500's one o'clock start. In honor of Memorial Day, we reached the pit lane to the music of the Purdue University Marching Band, followed by a flyover of vintage war planes, a military honor guard, and a motorcycle drill team. We carefully set up and tested the equipment for both pit areas as Florence Henderson sang "God Bless America." All the drivers were introduced by the track announcer, and at twelve forty-five p.m. we got the "Drivers to your cars" announcement.

It was almost show time. I put in my earplugs, started to pull on my flameproof hood, and then stopped and looked at my crew standing expectantly around the gleaming white car. In that moment, I realized that they were far more to me than just a pit crew. They had all battled through frustration and fear to get me to this exact moment, and I owed them a good run in the biggest race of them all. The prospect of getting crushed by G forces in an Indy car for the next three hours wasn't fun, but with the force of this team behind me, I was ready to push back. I went around the car to thank each one of them personally, unsuccessfully tried to get Sophie to stop crying, and received a fierce hug from Caroline.

"Is there anywhere else you'd rather be right now?" she asked as she released me.

"No. Well, maybe walking with you on a beach somewhere at midnight," I grinned.

"We'll do that later. Right now, Eddie, you go out

there and make us all proud."

I had a really clever reply ready, but it fell right out of my head as Caroline silenced me with a long kiss, which got the guys whistling and snickering in the background. All I could manage to do after that was nod and quickly pull my helmet on to cover my silly, embarrassed grin.

I slowly slid down into the tight-fitting seat and locked the steering wheel into place. Herb helped me buckle up the six-point safety harness as Rick plugged in my helmet radio and I pulled on my gloves. It was only then that I noticed a piece of silver tape in the middle of my steering wheel. I carefully peeled it back. Underneath was the design I had seen tattooed on Kevin's arm in the hospital back in England. It was King Arthur's sword, Excalibur, with wings on either side—the Apex logo. Neatly printed underneath it read,

Who Dares, Wins

Something to think about.

Finally, at exactly 1:01 p.m., the four words I'd been waiting six months to hear came over the track speakers, loud and clear.

"Gentlemen, start your engines!"

I found first gear as Rick and Herb gave me a push to get rolling, and I gently accelerated as the pack of thirty-three cars slowly got underway behind the silver Corvette pace car. The race hadn't even started but everyone was standing, clapping, and cheering loudly enough for me to hear the roar of the crowd over my engine.

Allan came on the radio.

"Pace car's pulling off, Edward. Two more warm-up laps. Remember, you have a very long afternoon ahead. Just play yourself in slowly. No heroics."

"OK. No hero stuff. Yet."

I was on the inside of the third row in seventh place and had a clear view of the starter as he waved the green flag and thirty-three drivers buried their throttles. The eleven neat rows of three disappeared into a boiling mass of cars shrieking into the first turn. I kept tight to the inside and had no plans to do anything other than keep my position and carefully build up to racing speed. Then the car in front of me started to slide to the right. That opened up a nice gap, and despite Allan's instructions, I reminded myself that I was paid to pass people.

I slipped by easily into sixth coming out of turn 2, tucked in behind the next guy all the way down the back straight, and darted to the inside going onto turn 3 for fifth place. Crossing the start/finish line for the first time, I was about two seconds back of the lead pack.

"Allan, who's up front?"

"Cerelli leading, then Carlos Molina, Scott Simon, and Ryan Burrell," Allan answered through my headset. "You're in fifth place. P5. Nice move, but remember to pace yourself."

Michael Cerelli had grown up in the shadow of the Indianapolis Speedway grandstands, and he'd won the 500 twice in the last four years. He was fast and smart—no wonder he was driving for one of the best teams in racing. Carlos Molina, on the other hand, was a Brazilian with Formula 1 experience starting his second Indy 500, and Scott Simon was an Indy rookie from California who had worked his way up through the bull rings of sprint car racing. Ryan Burrell was a champion sports car driver for the Audi factory team making his first start at Indy. They would be a tough group to crack.

"Edward?"

"Go ahead, Allan."

"Go to fuel position 3. Repeat, fuel position 3."

"OK. Going to fuel 3."

Stefan and I had started at position 4, and as Allan's plan was to save some fuel early in the race I knew what would happen when I clicked it down to 3. The engine would use less fuel, I'd have less power, and I'd be stuck in behind the lead group. For the next twenty-eight laps, I settled into a pace that produced lap times in the 218 to 220 mile-per-hour range. There were no lead changes up front, I always saw the same large group of cars behind me in my mirrors, lap after lap, and there were no accidents. Everyone was running very carefully, conserving fuel, holding whatever positions they had, and waiting for someone else to make the first move.

"Lap 29, Edward. One lap to—"

Allan's voice disappeared in the hiss of radio static.

Chapter 22

Under the Yellow Flag

"Allan! I lost you. Say again!"

"It's my heads—. Sorry. My headset, Edward. It's cutting in and out, for some reason. Pit in one lap, Edward. Pit in one. OK?"

"OK. Pit in one."

This would be our first pit stop under race conditions. No matter how many times we'd done it perfectly in practice, now it was for real. We were going to be doing this at least five more times so I hoped our first stop would be a clean, confidence-building one for the crew. A number of cars had gone in for their first pit stop on the previous lap, but Allan had kept me out to let the traffic clear. I peeled off the track smoothly after turn 3, slowed right down to sixty miles per hour as I entered the pit lane, and pulled the car to a stop right in front of Herb.

Instantly, Caroline snapped in the air hose and the

car jumped up on its onboard jacks. Rick locked in the fuel hose and began pumping in fuel as Kevin, James, Nigel, and Herb attacked the wheels with their air guns. I couldn't see behind very well, but I had a clear view of Nigel and Kevin as they changed the front wheels with lightning speed. Almost as suddenly as this frenzied activity began, it came to an end. I felt the car drop back down to the track on new tires as the air jack was released. In my left mirror, I saw Rick unlock and remove the fuel hose and watched Kevin and Nigel leap away from the front of the car.

"Go! Go! Go!" hollered Allan.

I selected first gear, gave the engine a lot of throttle, and spun the rear tires hard as I burned out of our pit and down the pit lane.

"Good stop, Allan!"

"Fuel and tires in a tick under fifteen seconds. They're not happy yet. You're on Lap 31. Running ninth."

I had lost four places to the rest of the field but some of those ahead of me still had to pit. With 169 laps left, I wasn't worried about getting back up near the front. I focused in on the eighth-place car in front of me and slowly began to close the gap. Five laps later, I was tucked in right behind him and looking to make a move going into turn 1.

I never got the chance.

"Yellow! Yellow! Back straight!" Allan yelled in my ear.

At the same moment, bright yellow lights flashed on around the track, and the safety workers waved their yellow flags furiously. There is a rainbow of colored flags and signal lights in racing, but yellow always means danger ahead. It commands drivers to slow down and form up in single file with no passing. I did exactly that, coasting through turn 2 and out onto the back straight.

Ryan Burrell's number forty-four car was jammed up hard against the outside wall. He had come out of turn 2 carrying too much speed, lost control, and slid up into the concrete. The impact had torn off everything on the right side of his car including both wheels, the suspension, and the rear wing. The track was littered with pieces of silver bodywork, metal, and carbon fiber.

"It's Burrell, Allan. Hit the wall out of 2. Lots of wreckage. It's going to stay yellow for a while."

Even though I'd just had a pit stop, Allan wanted to use the yellow flag caution period to check the car. After a big wreck there was always the chance of running over a sharp piece of wreckage on my second set of tires and damaging them. In a yellow-flag caution period, racing was suspended: I would maintain my position and there would be no penalty.

Every other team manager had the same idea, which resulted in a huge traffic jam of Indy cars all diving into their pits at the same time. Moments later, with fresh tires and more fuel, I emerged from the chaos of the pits.

"Allan, I'm back in line. How many more yellow laps?"

"Probably another five. The second set of tires is fine, no damage. We'll save them for later. Dial the fuel all the way down to 1 for now. Relax a bit and catch your breath. Good stop last time: 14.2 seconds. You're on lap 38."

I actually had six laps to sit back and think. The first thirty laps had been run without any incidents but after the first regular pit stop, drivers had started to get after each other and take some chances. Ryan Burrell took his best shot early and lost. His Indy 500 was over. Three other cars had also dropped out already with mechanical problems. I remembered what Allan had said about surviving the first 160 laps, being patient, and getting to the final stretch, ready to run those last 40 laps flat out.

At last, the green flag waved. I nailed the throttle, getting a good jump on the seventy-one car. I raced him side by side down the front straight, took the inside line into turn 1, and came out of it in eighth place.

For the next few laps, Stefan and I drove as a team, holding seventh and eighth places. But by the end of lap 58, my car had developed a "push" or understeer that made it difficult for me to maintain control. At the next pit stop, my team was able to fix the wings and solve the problem, but it had cost me a couple of places. Now running in twelfth, I had some ground to recover. And the struggle to maintain control had caused some severe discomfort around the metal plates in my ankle.

"Lots of time, Edward," Allan reminded me over the radio. "You're still on the lead lap and we're not even half way yet. Just give it a few laps and see how the car feels."

"It's way better, Allan. No push. Best it's been all day."

"Good. We're doing very well on fuel mileage. Go to 5 on the fuel mixture. Move up when you have the chance."

"OK. Going to fuel 5."

Better handling and a bit more power made an immediate difference. My ankle was less stressed, and I was able to catch cars again and work my way back up the running order over the next thirty laps. My next pit window was on lap 90, and by the time I came in for that stop I had climbed back up to eighth place. There were no wing adjustments this time: just fuel, tires, a quick drink, and Allan yelling "Go!"—all in just over thirteen seconds.

Another car ahead of me retired with a blown engine just before lap 100. At the halfway mark, I was back up to seventh and gaining on the lead pack ahead. In the middle of it, I saw Stefan's car right up in third, just behind Scott Simon. I gradually drew closer and eventually joined the tail end of this lead group of six cars as it snaked its way through traffic. Molina still led, but I had the best seat in the house to see Simon make a daring pass on the outside to take the lead and then begin to pull away.

Stefan was having a great run. He used that moment to make a move of his own on Molina. By the next lap, he was past him as well and up in second spot. Even though we were teammates in identical cars, Stefan was running his own race with his own strategy. Over the next twenty laps, I carefully set up two more passes and made my way into fifth. With both of his cars in the top five of the Indy 500, I could just imagine J.R. grinning ear to ear.

Chapter 23

A Very Costly Mistake

With that bit more power and the car handling so well, I was reluctant to come in as scheduled on lap 127 for fuel and tires. By this time, my crew had worked out any early race jitters. They were simply a blur as they darted around the car. I was out faster than ever before.

"Last pit: 12.9 seconds by my watch," Allan informed me. "Stay at fuel 6. Lap 128. P4."

Up ahead, Simon had a big lead on Stefan in second, who was just barely ahead of Molina. The heat rose in rippling waves from the track surface as we raced on into the hottest part of the day, and I fought back the pain from my ankle.

"Edward. Cerelli's coming up behind. Stay sharp."

I checked my left mirror and saw his yellow car gaining fast. Cerelli pulled inside and powered past, going into turn 3 in one smooth, fluid motion.

"Thanks, Allan. Where did he come from?"

"He lost time in the pits early. Bad battery. Let him go, Edward. He's down a lap from the leader. He's trying to get it back now."

But Cerelli, the hometown hero, was back in the hunt. Even though he had just passed Simon, Cerelli was still the last of ten cars on the lead lap: he had a very long way to go to catch up to the leaders again. Unless, of course, there was another yellow, in which case everyone would end up bunched together in single file behind the pace car. Then, whatever lead Simon had would disappear. But there was no yellow caution period to benefit Michael Cerelli or anyone else.

"Lap 158 coming up, Edward. At lap 160, we're into the last 100 miles. You're P4 with lots of fuel left. Exactly where you need to be. Go up to fuel 9 now. And watch for Cerelli. He's got the fastest car in the race, and he'll be back."

"OK. Going to fuel 9."

Simon, Stefan, and Molina all dove into the pits on the next lap to top up their fuel tanks and put on the best tires they had left. That briefly left Cerelli and me running second and first—but that couldn't last since both of us also had to stop once more to make it to the finish. The question was when.

"Edward?"

"Go, Allan."

"Go to fuel 10. Come in next lap. Repeat, pit next lap. Tires and a short fuel fill. OK?"

"OK. Fuel 10. Pit next lap."

I knew exactly what Allan was thinking. We had the fuel for full power, and I still had my second set of tires put aside, which had only done a few laps and had lots of wear left in them. Allan was going to bring me in to put on those tires and then "short fill" the fuel tank to fifteen gallons instead of the usual twenty-two. Carrying less fuel would save some weight and give me a touch more speed while still providing enough to run flat out to the finish with maximum power.

This was our last pit stop and by far the most important. Forcing the clutch pedal down, my ankle throbbed with a constant burning pain that traveled up my shaking leg. I knew that it would only be a few more seconds until Rick had finished with the fuel and unhooked the hose.

"Go! Go! Go!"

I revved the engine, thankfully released the clutch, and felt the back tires spin for an instant. Suddenly, I saw Nigel jump in front of the car, waving and yelling frantically. I slammed on the brakes, stopped the car dead, and stalled the engine. I had no idea what had happened until I looked in my left mirror and saw Rick struggling with the fuel hose.

It was still attached to the car.

With Kevin's help, Rick finally removed the hose. Then after several attempts, they restarted the engine.

"Go, Eddie! Go!" yelled a new voice that sounded oddly like J.R.'s.

I burned out of our pit for the last time and cruised slowly down the pit lane. Then I planted my foot to the floor as I snapped the car up through the gears and blended back onto the track. My head was spinning. What had gone wrong? Why was J.R. on the radio? This was not the carefully planned final pit stop that I thought would set us up for a fight to the finish.

Instead, we had just thrown it all away.

"Allan!"

I got no reply. I punched the transmit button again.

"Allan! Do you read?"

"I'm here, Edward. Go ahead."

"What happened?"

There was a short pause.

"A mistake. And it was not your fault. Put it aside. Understood?"

"OK. Understood."

"Good. Now listen closely, Edward. I've just been informed by the officials that we have to serve a drive-through penalty. Come back into the pits, but do not stop. Just drive through, watch your speed, and get back on the track. We'll lose some time but you will still be on the lead lap. OK?"

I had to pause and control my emotions before replying.

"OK. Got it."

I was far from OK. I'd read the Indianapolis rules carefully, and if a pit stop broke any of those rules, the officials slapped the offending team with a range of penalties. Leaving the pit with the fuel hose still attached to the car absolutely broke the rules, and the penalty for that was harsh. You had to come right back in again and drive through the pit lane at 60 miles per hour while your competition stayed out on the track, lapping at 225.

I slowed down and came off the track again, drove through the pit lane, and caught a fleeting glimpse of my crew as they just stood there looking shattered. I got back on the track and accelerated up to racing speed on lap 182. If my last pit stop had gone as planned, I should have been right back with Stefan and the rest of the lead group, but they were nowhere in sight.

"Edward. You are the last car on the lead lap. Simon's in first, then Stefan, Molina, and Cerelli in a tight group. You are twenty-four seconds behind, running in fifth. Lap 183."

As a rookie in the Indy 500, fifth place was nothing to be ashamed of. But I also knew that, after the race we'd had, settling for fifth felt like a cop-out. Then and there, I decided that if I only had seventeen laps left, I was going to make each one of them a statement about what our team could do. But in the back of my mind, I knew that we were out of options and out of time.

We needed more than pure speed—we needed some pure luck.

Chapter 24

Who Dares, Wins

"Yellow! Yellow! Yellow! Turn 3!"

Allan's shouting exploded inside my helmet as I was exiting turn 2 and entering the back straight. The yellow lights flashed and I carefully eased out of the throttle. I knew Allan was watching the lead group ahead of me from the pit TV.

"Allan! Talk to me!"

"Molina brushed the wall in turn 3! He's pulled off into the pits. He's finished. But we have a yellow, Edward! A yellow! You're on lap 190. Ten to go. You're in fourth place now. Close up!"

"Roger that!"

That yellow flag changed everything! Indy is famous for some unexpected last minute events that can turn the race upside down, and I was right in the middle of this one. As I arrived at turn 3, I saw what Allan had described. Carlos Molina's car was crawling slowly into the pits after he had pushed too hard, lost control, and brushed it up against the wall. He hadn't hit hard enough to tear up the car, but he had certainly damaged it enough so that he couldn't continue.

I scanned the track ahead for any pieces of wreckage, but didn't see anything that would need a lot of cleaning up by the track crews. They would sweep and inspect the accident area to be certain, but this caution period was likely to be a short one. And it was exactly what I needed to close the gap on the leaders.

The Corvette pace car came out again on lap 191, and the field formed up behind it in single file, circulating slowly until the officials were satisfied that the track was safe to resume racing. I closed right up into fourth spot, directly behind Simon, Stefan, and Cerelli. Once the official waved the green flag, I was back in contention.

"Hey, Allan!"

"Go ahead, Edward."

"Is anyone up front coming in?"

"Not yet. I'm watching their pits. I'll let you know. Just breathe. Focus."

"OK."

"Edward. One more thing."

"Go, Allan."

"The mistake at the last pit stop. It was my fault. Not yours. I told you to go too early. I thought I could get you out in front of Molina. I was wrong. I wanted you to know that."

Aside from my dad, there was no one I respected more than Allan Tanner, and right then I knew why.

"Thanks for that, Allan. I mean it. But you know what? It doesn't matter. We've still got a shot."

"Yes, we do. So listen to me now, Edward. We have one last chance, and this is the Indianapolis 500. If you only ever win one more race, make it this one."

The atmosphere in the stadium was electric. As the tension built, I had to use all of my concentration to stay focused. The slower speed of the caution period gave me an extra second to scan the steering wheel. There, the small Apex design and motto caught my attention: *Who Dares, Wins.*

I flexed my fingers around the steering wheel for a moment and smiled, feeling a renewed surge of my old confidence.

And why not? I had a great car that could run 228. I had three cars to pass and five laps to do it. It would all come down to how fast I could fight my way through to challenge for the lead. There was no time left for carefully planned race strategies or complicated passing maneuvers. It looked like the only way past the three guys ahead was to go straight at them.

The Corvette pace car peeled off the track for the last time as we entered the front straight and Scott Simon was already hard on it, streaking up to 220 as he led Stefan, Cerelli, and me across the line to take the green flag, bunched nose to tail. I stayed right under Cerelli's rear wing through turns 1 and 2 and down the back straight, watching every movement of his car and how it was handling.

Cerelli had been forced to drive flat out for most of the race to claw his way back onto the lead lap, and he was paying for it now with a tired race car on worn tires. Where my car was rock solid through the turns, his was a real handful. It darted nervously left and right while he tried to hold it in the groove. Halfway down the back straight, he topped out at 225 and I made my move, darting out from behind and going by on the inside, taking third place as we entered turn 3.

Michael Cerelli had run the 500 six times and won it twice; he knew exactly how to play this game. He immediately tucked in right behind me through turn 4, hoping to pick up the draft and put the same move on me as we entered the front straight. But he didn't have 800 EuroTech horsepower under his right foot like I did, and I steadily pulled away as my speed increased to 228 and lap 197 began.

Four laps to go. I caught up to Stefan and Simon on the back straight and watched for an opening as they were locked in a battle for the lead. Stefan's elfish appearance and his cheerful nature didn't inspire an image of him as a tough competitor, but watching him go wheel to wheel with Simon reminded me just how ferocious the little guy could be in a race car. He made his move as the two of them entered turn 3, only to have Simon squeeze him down into the low groove and protect his lead. Stefan came right back at him in turn 4 and took the lead coming onto the main straight, only to have Simon pass him again crossing the line, and hold him off as they arced into turn 1 again.

Three to go. I stayed a few car lengths behind the two of them and slowed a touch to 225 as I studied their cars, looking for a weakness. Like mine, Stefan's car was smooth and solid, thanks to our aero package. Simon's car was dancing dangerously on the edge of disaster, and he had it right on the limit to keep Stefan at bay. A quick glance in my mirror confirmed that Cerelli had again narrowed the gap behind me, but I kept my focus on the two cars in front as they ran side by side and traded the lead three more times before we completed the lap. I knew that I had speed in reserve, but I needed some racing room to use it. So far they hadn't given me an inch.

Two to go. Stefan led Simon through the first two turns and onto the back straight, but when I checked my left mirror to make sure of Cerelli's position, I was startled to see nothing but empty track. No bright yellow car. I shot a glance at my right mirror and there he was, edging alongside between my car and the concrete wall on a course that would put him in the high groove for turn 3. At the same time, Simon had also darted out to the right, setting himself up in the same high groove as a way to get around Stefan on the outside. I thought both of them had lost their minds, running that close to the wall at 225 miles per hour.

No one risked that high groove if there was room anywhere else. But as Cerelli and I had no good racing room ahead, he had decided to try and find some up high. I didn't know if Simon had the same idea or if he planned to put the squeeze on Stefan, but we were all fast approaching turn 3, spread across the width of the track. Four cars weren't going to make it into that turn. As the leader, Stefan needed to back off, or go low to give Simon some room before he slid up into the wall.

At the last moment, Stefan took the low groove into the turn, allowing Simon to ease away from the wall. I tucked in tight behind and followed. Stefan held onto the lead, I slotted into second and Cerelli swooped down into third taking the middle groove. Simon found himself a distant fourth after he was forced to slow down to avoid sliding up into the wall. We came out of turn 4 and onto the main straight that way as we got the white flag from the starter.

The white flag—one lap to go. At last, I thought, I'd have some racing room ahead—but before I could move out from behind Stefan, Cerelli was there again, passing us both for the lead going into turn 1 for the final time. Stefan and I tucked in behind him in second and third through turn 2, and then we hit the back straight. The only advantage I had over Cerelli and Stefan was my higher straight-line speed, and this would be my last chance to use it. I knew that they would top out at 225, and that I could run 228. With enough room, I might be able to overhaul them both.

Even though Stefan and I had identical cars, they were set up differently. Stefan liked to run a little more wing than I did. This helped him in the corners but cut his top speed by a few miles per hour. I was running less wing and also carrying less fuel, an advantage Allan had given me with a short fill on my final stop. Those differences added to my top speed, but it still wouldn't be enough to get me past two cars in the space of the back straight.

So I did the one thing racing drivers never do. I backed off.

Chapter 25

Kiss the Bricks

I had the combined length of the back straight, the last two corners, and half of the main straight to build up to top speed and then sling-shot past both Stefan and Cerelli before the finish line.

It was only a slight lift of the throttle for a second, but it got me into their draft and opened a gap between us. I waited for them to dive into turn 3, and then I nailed it, accelerating hard back into the gap, building up momentum, and hauling them in fast as they raced each other out of turn 3. There is a very short straight between turns 3 and 4 where I hit 228 and pulled alongside Stefan. He was so focused on Cerelli that he didn't expect me to be there, especially accelerating past on the inside to take second place and the fast line into the final turn.

Cerelli's car was a few lengths ahead as we went

through turn 4 for the last time, but I was carrying more speed as we raced flat out to the finish. I edged alongside his car, watched our front wheels draw even, and wondered how much road was left ahead. There was no doubt that I was passing him, and if I'd timed my slingshot move exactly right, I'd take the lead just before we hit the finish line. If not, Michael Cerelli would have his third Indianapolis 500 victory. And I'd be the guy who finished a really close second—and whom no one would remember.

The starter furiously waved the checkered flag. For an instant, I saw the finish line in the middle of a three-foot wide strip of red bricks before it flashed under my car. And then it was all over. Cerelli and I crossed the line almost side by side, but from my vantage point it was too close to tell who had won. The only thing for certain was that the margin of victory could have been no more than the nose of an Indy car.

Allan's voice exploded inside my helmet.

"Eddie! Fantastic! Eddie! You—"

Then nothing. Allan's voice was cut off again. Of all the moments for the radio glitches to return! I'd never heard Allan that excited. And it was the first time he had ever called me Eddie. I hit my radio button.

"Hey, Allan!"

All I got was a steady hiss of radio static.

"Allan! Anyone! Come in! Who won?"

Still nothing.

As I continued to coast slowly through turns 1 and 2 of the cool-down lap, I flipped up my helmet visor, drank in the cool air, and heard the roar of the enormous crowd. They were on their feet screaming, clapping, and cheering. Cerelli, Stefan, Simon, and I had certainly given them their money's worth, but who were they cheering for?

Our speed had been reduced to a walking pace and I saw a massive crowd of officials, race team members, and media people waiting just ahead. Michael Cerelli pulled in behind my car as we rolled to a stop and shut down our engines. A large group of beaming officials in bright yellow shirts surrounded my car. The biggest of them leaned into the cockpit and yelled over the crowd noise.

"Just one more left turn today, son. You can park it right in there!"

The officials pushed my car from behind. As it rolled ahead, the crowd parted and I turned left into the best place at the Indianapolis Motor Speedway.

Victory Lane.

"I can't believe that anyone would need more photos,"

I said. "I'm sure they took thousands in Victory Lane and at the awards banquet last night."

Throughout the entire next day, I relived the memory of the moments after the race. I remembered the crowds and the cheers—and Caroline's big kiss on national TV, as promised—but the whole experience was overwhelming.

Over the years, I'd watched hundreds of races on TV, and the post-race interviews of the winner are always the same. The TV guy stands there with a microphone and asks the same set of "So how was it out there?" questions. And the drivers always answer with the standard lame line about how well their sponsor's car ran and how awesome their crew was. I had always dreamed of having the chance to be interviewed after a big race win—and of having something much more original and interesting to say.

But, in the end, after we left Victory Lane, all I could remember saying was that the DynaSport car ran great all day and that my crew was awesome. Because they really were.

"These are the official Speedway photos, Eddie," Caroline replied, interrupting my thoughts. "Team shots with the winning car. And, of course, we kiss the bricks."

The DynaSport team stood patiently on the finish

line beside our winning car while the official photos were taken the next morning. As Caroline had promised, the first picture required us to kneel down and kiss the narrow strip of the original speedway bricks saved from the very first race in 1909 and inlaid at the start/finish line. After that one, we lined up and smiled on command, but believe me—no one was faking it for the cameras. Our wide grins were for real.

"Take a good look around, Eddie," Rick said as he scanned the massive speedway. "Not too bad for a couple of guys from west Vancouver. So, what are you going to do with your share of the prize money?"

"I am finally going to take Caroline out to dinner," I replied immediately. "Somewhere nice. Without you."

"Like where?" Caroline asked.

"I don't know," I replied. "You love fresh grilled seafood. How about Australia?"

"Not so fast," Rick said. "Just because you won the 500, it doesn't mean that you get to take off to the other side of the world with my sister."

Caroline laughed. "There are plenty of great restaurants in Indianapolis, Eddie," she said. "And you are absolutely taking me to one of them tonight. And yes, without my older brother, thanks very much. Then I have to finish editing my film about all of this and hand it in by next week. While I'm doing that you need to get your ankle looked after."

I'd learned how to deal with G forces but when Caroline took charge, I had no chance.

"And after all that, Mr. Stewart, you can start returning your phone calls," Rick said. "I checked the messages on the answering machine this morning. There's a bunch of people who want to talk to you."

"No way, Rick. I absolutely cannot do another interview," I replied. "I'm even boring myself now."

"Well," Rick stated. "You might be a boring guy to interview—actually you *are* a boring guy to interview—but you've won the Indianapolis 500, Eddie Stewart. That changes things. Suddenly, you're the guy who can win the big one. And we're your team. I think we're going to be very busy, my friend."

Caution period. A point when the race is slowed to allow the track to be cleared. Signaled by a yellow flag.

Computational Fluid Dynamics (CFD). One of the branches of fluid mechanics. It uses mathematics to help analyze how a solid object behaves when it moves through the air or through water.

Data acquisition. A computer system that collects information on race car performance.

Downforce. The load placed on a car by air flow over its front and rear WINGS.

Formula Atlantic. A single-seat, open-wheeled race car.

G force. One G is equal to the normal force of gravity on your body.

Gearbox. Contains gears that the driver shifts to transmit engine power to the wheels.

Grid. The starting lineup of cars, which is based upon qualifying times.

Grip. The amount of traction a car's tires has at any given point. It affects the driver's ability to keep control through corners.

Indy car. An Indianapolis-style, single-seat, open-wheeled racing car.

Marshals. Racetrack safety workers.

Oversteer. When the rear wheels lose their GRIP and a race car slides or spins.